DANGEROUS
Gentlemen

by

BEVERLEY OAKLEY

Ordering Information:
Quantity sales. Special discounts are available on quantity purchases by corporations, associations, and others. For details, contact the "Special Sales Department" at the address above.

Dangerous Gentlemen/Beverley Oakley –2nd ed.
ISBN 978-1523687411

For Bernie and Nina

Chapter One

BRUSHING BEETLES OUT of her cleavage as she shrouded herself in the fronds of a concealing potted palm was not how Hetty envisaged making her grand London debut.

Still, it was better to be *hidden* by the flamboyant greenery than to be humiliated like…a wallflower, she thought, trying to suppress her growing agitation at how tonight had fallen so short of her expectations for the grand event she'd envisaged.

Of course, she *had* prepared herself for such a fate. She truly thought that having lived in the shadow of her beautiful sister for the past eighteen years had inured her to social disappointment.

Yet, being passed over for the last four dances at Lady Knox's lavish ball this evening had brought home to her that, indeed, the reality was far, far worse than just worrying about it.

A painful reality that was going to last another three months before she could return to her quiet, unexciting but familiar home in the country.

As the orchestra tuned up for another country dance, Hetty watched the slow progress of a ladybird over the bodice of her white sarcenet gown. How much more complementary the little creature's bold red-and-black coat was to her own lackluster coloring. A debutante was required to wear white and pale shades to reflect her innocence, status and wealth. The ballroom was bursting with such rare prizes, she reflected gloomily as she carefully transferred the ladybird onto a palm frond. Wallflowers like Hetty faced fierce competition and she was not bolstered by her sister Araminta's kind reassurance that her sizeable dowry would ultimately compensate for her lack of looks.

Guiltily she watched her chaperone Mrs. Monks pass nearby, an anxious frown turning down the corners of her thin, bloodless mouth. Hetty held her breath. The truth was, she wasn't hiding only to avoid public humiliation. Or her chaperone.

Really, she was here to spy, though spying was the preserve of devious sorts like Araminta.

Araminta, the bold and beautiful sister who was currently clasping hands with the handsome baronet whose brief kindness toward Hetty at the beginning of the evening had ignited a torrent of never-before-experienced sensations. Unfortunately, his later actions had quashed every hope for the season Hetty had foolishly entertained.

No, spying from behind a potted palm was as close as a shy, plump debutante like Hetty would ever get to her heart's desire.

A little sob escaped her as she gazed upon the well-matched couple. Araminta, as always, was dazzling. Yet for a few moments earlier this evening, dressed for her first ball in her lovely silk gown with its powder-blue sash, her light-brown hair tumbling in curls from a high topknot at the apex of a center parting, Hetty, too, had felt almost beautiful.

Then Araminta had swept her aside to admire her own gleaming reflection before the looking glass.

Indeed, gleaming and self-satisfied were appropriate epithets, and ones Hetty was as inclined to use on the family Siamese cat as her sister. She knew she shouldn't be uncharitable. Araminta's first season had ended under a cloud and she knew she should be pleased her sister had caught the eye of a man as seriously handsome and eligible as Sir Aubrey, a baronet who was set to inherit a viscountcy and vast estates in the north.

But it was hard to rejoice in Araminta's good fortune when Hetty still felt the pain of her sister's dismissive, "I suppose you're up to the mark as much as can be expected". Hetty should have known better than to ask for an opinion on her appearance.

Not only had tonight brought home how wanting Hetty was in the eyes of the male contingent, it had highlighted how beneath the notice of dashing Sir Aubrey she was. Yet the evening had started on such a high note when Sir Aubrey had returned her dropped reticule to her with a bow of sweeping chivalry and a smile that had seemed for her alone. Silly girl. He smiled like that at all the girls, of course.

Still, Hetty never suffered from the blue devils for long and the lively music soon had her tapping her feet, enjoying her seclusion and fascinated by the way the light caught the extraordinary streak of white hair that cut a swathe through Sir Aubrey's dark locks. Araminta, while pointing out the peculiarities of several gentlemen of interest, had told her earlier in the evening that it was a physical trait shared by all the men in his family.

The foot-tapping stopped abruptly when Hetty saw Araminta stumble, causing Sir Aubrey to tighten his hold.

Conniving minx, Hetty thought uncharitably, even though being charitable was, she knew, one of her few commendable traits, and if she couldn't be beautiful she should at least try to be nice.

Living with Araminta, however, had opened her eyes to the fact that vibrant beauties could get away without being nice or charitable, and Araminta was certainly neither. But in all those years, Hetty had not known jealousy.

The corrosive poison had only started dripping into her veins tonight. Of course, she was used to seeing her sister feted, admired and in continual demand. But it was hard to witness Sir Aubrey's interest, even though she'd told herself a thousand times it should not come as a surprise that rakish, handsome Sir Aubrey didn't notice debutantes like plain, plump and awkward Hetty.

His piercing smile at the beginning of the evening had been an aberration. That had been made very clear when an hour ago he'd accidentally spilled champagne upon her arm yet barely paused to flick a snowy linen handkerchief across her sleeve and offer a lackluster apology before hurrying on.

Standing on tiptoe to get a better view through the glossy leaves of her concealment, Hetty was relieved to see Sir Aubrey was no longer dancing with Araminta, though it was hardly consoling to see him partnering another beautiful brunette.

Especially when, in the midst of conversation, he brushed a lock of the young woman's hair back from her face.

The intimacy of the gesture, or rather the look upon his face, sent tendrils of pain and pleasure deep into Hetty's belly, though these hitherto alien bodily experiences turned to fright when a familiar growl warmed her ear at the same time as the speaker delivered her a playful slap upon the rump.

"Who, may I ask, Hetty dearest, has caught your discerning eye this evening? Tell me so that I might facilitate the joyful union before season's end. You know I've made it my mission to see to your happiness."

Hetty whirled 'round, blinking up at her cousin Stephen,

unsure whether pity, amusement or—God forbid—scorn would be his response when she offered her almost guilty admission as to the object of her interest.

To her surprise, it was horror. Horror delivered with surely unnecessary force, given that all of London knew Sir Aubrey Banks was a prime catch. She'd heard him discussed in such terms by more than one designing mama.

Although, registering Cousin Stephen's antipathy, Hetty reflected that there had been some caveat about Sir Aubrey's eligibility whispered in an undertone by her mama's friend Mrs. Dobson.

Stephen's earlier good humor evaporated and he looked pained. "My dear Hetty, lose your heart to *anyone* but Sir Aubrey," he exhorted her. "Under no circumstances can he be a candidate for your affections." Suspicion laced his next question. "He hasn't spoken to you, has he?" Stephen put his hands on her shoulders, a troubled crease between his brows. What she'd thought anger was, she now realized, the gravest concern.

"He's never looked twice at me, Cousin Stephen, and why would he? I'm in no danger from his advances." Hetty sought for the word she'd heard whispered in the drawing room in the months preceding her come-out. A word she knew no innocent debutante ought to know. "Is he a philanderer?"

Stephen returned to his natural height with a look that was part wry amusement, part censure. "No, Sir Aubrey is not a renowned philanderer, but what he is must not concern you." He became brisk. "Since it would appear you are not taken for the quadrille that is forming, perhaps you'd do me the honor?"

A passing debutante being hurried along by her chaperone cast Hetty an envious look as Hetty slipped her hand into the crook of her cousin's arm. Her confidence was returning. Not only was darling Cousin Stephen the most amenable of men, he was extraordinarily handsome. Hetty wondered why, after all these months in London, his eye had not yet been caught by some dashing creature, though she reasoned he'd want to wait the few months until it was known if he'd remain heir to The Grange. That hinged on whether the child soon to be born to Hetty's mama, Lady Partington, was a boy, in which case the infant would displace Cousin Stephen.

But if Mama had a girl, it was unlikely at her age she'd have more children and then Cousin Stephen would remain Lord Partington's heir.

Hetty hoped that would be the case. If Cousin Stephen became the new viscount, he'd surely be charitable to Hetty during the long, lonely years of spinsterhood that stretched before her.

A great sense of security enveloped her when, with a brotherly smile, he patted her hand.

Cousin Stephen had caused quite a stir when he'd first arrived at The Grange a few months earlier, for Araminta had set out with determination to snare the affections of the heir to her ancestral home. She'd lost interest, however, when Cousin Stephen's future was thrown in doubt.

Or rather, Stephen had lost interest in Araminta.

It didn't matter now. Araminta was determined to make a glittering match, Stephen's future would remain unknown for some months and Hetty looked set to finish her first season in glorious ignominy, perhaps standing up to dance only when Cousin Stephen took pity on her.

As Hetty took her place beside Stephen, she sent her sister, who was partnering an aging and apparently gout-ridden peer, as smug a look as she dared, under the circumstances. The ballroom was crowded and Araminta, who was adept at swift revenge, would understand Hetty's inference. Araminta was the queen of set-downs and Hetty had to assert herself when she could.

She was amused and a little relieved when her sister puckered her full mouth in mock adoration of the poor specimen beside her. If Araminta was able to make a joke of it, perhaps her good humor would last through the evening and she'd be less inclined to harp upon Hetty's lack of success.

Perhaps Hetty might even find she'd enjoyed herself by the end of the evening too. It was, after all, the grandest occasion she'd ever attended. Hundreds of beeswax candles cast a lustrous glow upon the assembled finery and the music and the food were of the highest quality.

As they waited to perform their steps, Hetty murmured, "You have not said, Cousin Stephen, why I should be wary of Sir Aubrey. If you have any knowledge of young ladies, you'd know your cautions are likely to have the opposite effect to that desired. Surely any designing mama would be perfectly delighted to see her daughter waltz off with such a handsome, rich gentleman of consequence?"

Stephen linked elbows with her for the next dance sequence, his lips set in a grim line. "This is no time for such a discussion, Hetty. Sir Aubrey is not the gentleman he presents to the rest of the world. Pray don't concern yourself with a scoundrel like him when there's a roomful of eligible young men who'd be only too delighted to further their acquaintance with you."

This was hardly consolation, Hetty reflected. Good-natured Stephen had grown increasingly serious since taking up his position in the Foreign Office, though he clearly enjoyed the new responsibilities he'd assumed with the backing of his cousin, Hetty's father. Viscount Partington was obviously fond of Stephen and had pulled strings to secure a position he believed would engage Stephen's mind if he were to be ousted as heir.

"A scoundrel?" Hetty scanned the crowd for another glimpse of the gentleman who'd grown even more fascinating since Stephen's strictures. With an unexpected pang, she found him partnering exactly the kind of bold and strikingly pretty young lady she would expect. Her gaze lingered on his mouth, lips pressed together almost grimly until his features were suddenly reordered by a moment's animation, his dark- brown eyes lighting up and his lips curving to reveal good, strong teeth. When he brushed his hand across his elegantly chiseled sideburns to rake back his springy dark hair, cut short on the sides and worn longer and slightly brushed forward on top, Hetty shivered, completely in thrall.

Before she'd come to London, the only men she'd known were country squires and their uninspiring sons and...Cousin Edgar.

With sadness, she remembered her old playmate, kind but doltish Edgar, who'd died in a boating accident some months before. She'd believed the affection had been mutual until Araminta had lured him away with no more than the crook of her little finger.

"Surely I'm allowed to cast my gaze upon him?" She spoke softly and was ashamed at the longing in her voice as she looked up into her cousin's pitying eyes.

Stephen smiled and tucked a lock of hair behind her ear. "I can't stop you but perhaps if I entrust you with a great secret—one I would reveal to no one else—it might temper your adolescent fantasies." With a surreptitious glance at their neighbors waiting, like them, to perform their steps, he put his mouth to her ear and whispered, "Sir Aubrey is a suspected Spencean…a traitor to king and crown. If he's convicted, you know what penalty that carries."

Instead of rewarding this damning statement with the no-doubt horror expected, Hetty squared her shoulders. "Then why is he not awaiting trial?"

"Securing evidence is my job." Stephen looked uncomfortable. "If that's not sufficient to damn him in your eyes, then I must speak with a frankness I would ordinarily not employ when addressing an innocent debutante."

"Really, Cousin Stephen, you're sounding more and more like some pompous and important man of government than my cousin. I have no delicate sensibilities. I simply want to know how an apparently *persona non grata*—if that's the right term—can be allowed to rub shoulders with the *haute ton* and dance with…innocent debutantes like me. Surely if his reputation is so fearful, he'd have been forcibly removed by the very supercilious butler who greeted us?"

Stephen looked unimpressed. Lowering his head, he muttered, "Don't shriek, then, Hetty, when I tell you that Sir Aubrey was married to a woman who became so fearful of him she ran away to seek refuge with her cousin, the new Viscount Debenham, as he's become known since his recent inheritance."

He gripped Hetty more tightly as he danced her down the room beneath an arch of fellow dancers' arms, emerging to add, "When Sir Aubrey went after his wife, Lady Margaret, she took her own life, leaving a letter outlining the full extent of Sir Aubrey's evil associations and crimes."

"Oh." Hetty swallowed. This was not at all what she'd expected. Distracted, she waited in line for the next part of the dance, her gaze returning to the dangerous gentleman who so fascinated her and who was now partnering his lovely consort beneath the arches. "Then why was the letter not sufficient to condemn him?"

Another look of discomfort flitted across Stephen's face. He cleared his throat. "It has gone missing. Lord Debenham, or Mr. George Carruthers as he was formerly, informed Foreign Office of the contents of his cousin's letter. He'd found it clutched in the late Lady Margaret's hand but said that after leaving the room to seek assistance, the letter had disappeared when he returned. He believes it was stolen by a retainer, perhaps ignorant of its importance, who planned to gain by it through blackmail."

Shaken, Hetty clasped Stephen's hand for the final steps of the dance. "And has that happened? Has he been blackmailed? When did Lady Margaret die?"

"Eighteen months ago. And no, to date there has been no sign of the letter." Hetty smiled but the force of Stephen's response tempered her smugness.

"Keep your distance, Hetty. I've told you only what I believe appropriate for a girl of your delicacy, but there's more." Coming up from his bow at the conclusion of the dance, he added, "Those who fall foul of Sir Aubrey have not all lived to tell the tale."

* * *

A traitor. The words chased themselves around Hetty's head as Stephen led her toward the lackluster Mrs. Monks, a youngish widow and, like Hetty, not possessed of the kinds of qualities likely to inspire the passion Lady Margaret clearly had inspired in her male admirers.

So when Araminta sidled up to her sister to mention in her usual patronizing manner that Hetty had what appeared to be a poppy seed between her teeth, Hetty was glad of the excuse to scuttle away to the sanctuary afforded by her friendly, luxuriant potted palm to pick at the elusive poppy seed—which she soon suspected never existed. Resuming her earlier occupation, she gazed from amidst the greenery upon Sir Aubrey, in earnest discussion with two gentlemen Cousin Stephen had pointed out as government ministers.

How handsome and urbane he looked; how charming his manner. The thrill that curdled in her lower belly was followed by suspicion as she reviewed Stephen's possible motives for damning his character.

Did he fear the man might break her heart? That Hetty was so bird-witted, painting him black would make inevitable rejection easier for her?

Sir Aubrey was everything Hetty would have thought she'd find repugnant in a man. He was immaculate with an edge of danger that unsettled her. Some might say his confidence verged on arrogance. He could not be more different from poor Edgar.

And yet for some inexplicable reason he set her pulse racing, made her throat dry and sent the heat to her cheeks every time he even looked in her direction.

Not that his few glances registered either his chivalry at the start of the evening or his painful disregard partway through. He simply looked right through her.

She was safely out of the gentleman's orbit and always would be. Sir Aubrey consorted with bold beauties he never married. Not pale, plump and wilting wallflowers like Hetty.

Eventually the night was at an end. Hetty had been counting down the hours as increments of torture, but Araminta was positively glowing with success as she climbed into the carriage beside her sister for their return home.

"It's a shame you didn't dance with Sir Aubrey as I did— twice—Hetty dearest, for that might have livened up your spirits. When you look as glum as you do now, I'm reminded of last night's roly-poly pudding sitting on my plate with two currants staring at me, just like your eyes." Araminta's pretty white teeth gleamed in the light of a street lamp above her ivory fan as she went on to reflect on her own success. "Mr. Minchin came to claim me for my second quadrille just as Sir Aubrey arrived to ask me. Well, you won't believe what happened."

Although Hetty evinced no desire to find out, Araminta breezed on. "Sir Aubrey said he'd waive the fifty pounds Mr. Minchin still owed him from a game of faro the night before if Mr. Minchin waived his claim to his dance with me."

Araminta's eyes glittered. "Of course, it wasn't very chivalrous of Mr. Minchin to agree, was it, though who would you have preferred to partner you, Hetty? Mr. Minchin or Sir Aubrey?"

It was a rhetorical question, Hetty knew. Araminta did not concern herself with other people's desires unless they ran counter to her own, in which case she was assiduous in trampling them. Hetty knew that to her cost. Still, like the dutiful sister she was, she murmured, "Sir Aubrey, I'm sure. He must admire you very much."

"Indeed he does." Araminta gazed thoughtfully at the carriage roof, unconsciously licking her lips. "He is a very good catch. Though only a baronet, he is in line for a viscountcy and to inherit large landholdings in Wiltshire. His country seat would be the grandest for a hundred miles, I'm told. And of course, he's very handsome. I couldn't consider a husband who wasn't."

Bravely, Hetty said softly, "You didn't think Edgar was

handsome."

She was not surprised when Araminta scoffed with no concern for her sister's feelings. "Edgar was going to be master of The Grange. It didn't matter what he looked like, for you know my greatest desire has always been to be mistress of my beloved family home." She sniffed, her expression suddenly tragic, and for a moment Hetty thought she was at least paying lip service to the grief she should feel at poor Edgar's untimely death. Instead, Araminta's tone was bitter. "Now Mama's *enceinte* and if our new sibling is a boy then he will inherit. If we get a sister and Cousin Stephen inherits, Cousin Stephen's reluctance to marry me just because I'm his cousin forces me to make my way in the world as best I can." A satisfied smile banished her grief as she pronounced, "I just can't make up my mind whether to set my sights on Sir Aubrey or the new Lord Debenham."

Gloomily, Hetty reflected that Araminta was just the kind of dazzling beauty who apparently appealed to Sir Aubrey. "Sir Aubrey is not looking for a wife, I'm told." Hetty looked combative. "He's said to enjoy dalliances, though."

"A handsome gentleman like Sir Aubrey is bound to be regarded with jealousy and to have detractors."

"Of whom Lord Debenham is one."

Araminta raised her eyebrows. "You know a lot for someone who only danced with our cousin." She settled herself more comfortably against the squabs and smiled. "If you're so good at ferreting out such information, perhaps you won't be entirely useless this season after all."

Chapter Two

THE LIFE OF a debutante is a busy one, regardless of how successful she is. Araminta was in demand for her walks and shopping expeditions with various "bosom buddies" she'd made during her ten short days in London. Agreeing to all and sundry with enthusiasm, she informed Hetty and Stephen that her popularity with these young ladies was due to their hope Araminta's loveliness would draw the young men into their general orbit.

For Hetty, life was no less busy, as their chaperone Mrs. Monks decided Hetty's lack of success could be ameliorated by assiduous training in the art of deportment and associated graces.

So while Araminta shopped and promenaded, Hetty paced the drawing room with half a dozen books balanced on her head and a long wooden ruler inserted between her stays and her chemise.

Dubiously, Mrs. Monks finally declared Hetty as ready as she'd ever be for the grand ball that was being held to mark the debut of the lovely and vivacious Miss Felicity Pangbourne.

Hetty had, by this stage, lost all interest in the social events that inspired such excitement and confident expectation in her sister. They merely reinforced Hetty's inadequacy. Even the knowledge that Sir Aubrey's attendance was assured, since he was currently Mr. Pangbourne's houseguest, could not jolt her out of her gloom.

By the time the carriage drew up in front of the fine London townhouse on the night of the ball, Hetty's spirits were at their lowest ebb.

"What do you wager that either Sir Aubrey or Lord Debenham will ask me to dance three times this evening?" Araminta asked coquettishly as the girls stepped out of the carriage and mounted the stairs toward the double doors being held open by two footmen.

"Neither will, for it's tantamount to making you an offer, which they won't on such limited acquaintance."

Araminta fanned herself languidly as she contemplated this. "Oh, I know Sir Aubrey well enough…" She could barely contain her secret excitement as she added, "But I intend to know him a great deal better before the evening is over."

Stephen, who had accompanied his cousins due to Mrs. Monks' taking ill at the last moment, looked dark as he stepped aside to let the girls pass into the ballroom. "You be sure to convey to your silly sister that Sir Aubrey is one gentleman she must steer clear of," he murmured in Hetty's ear.

"You'd better tell her, for she won't listen to me," responded Hetty as the warmth of the crowded room enveloped her, making her shiver with apprehension.

Cousin Stephen harrumphed. "I mentioned my concern in the mildest terms, for the last thing I want is to whip up Araminta's interest. She might take it as a challenge. However, judging by that long face of yours, I'd wager you aren't averse to a little attention from out-of-bounds quarters either. Well, for once, Hetty, I'm glad you're not in any danger."

"Because I'm plain and frumpy?"

Ignoring this as he led the girls to a relatively secluded corner, he responded smoothly, "Shy and self-effacing, which is far more appealing. Sir Aubrey prefers young ladies like your sister and I wish I'd spoken earlier to Araminta as you're right, she's hardly likely to heed your warnings."

"Not where a handsome gentleman is concerned," muttered Hetty, fiddling with her fan. She looked up. "I still haven't heard anyone else speak ill of him with the vigor you do."

"That's because I work for the Foreign Office and they don't." His tone gentled. "Please, Hetty, I want you wed to someone worthy of you. You are so like your mother." To Hetty's surprise his expression gentled even more. "You need to be nurtured. I know things about Sir Aubrey I cannot tell you."

Hetty stared at the points of her dancing slippers peeking from beneath the rose- flounced hem of her cream-and-gold sarcenet, with its tiny gauze sleeves. She truly had felt like a fairy princess as Jane had helped her dress this evening. Pearls were woven into her hair and she'd thought her face more sculpted and her complexion improved since she'd come to London. Then Araminta had commented that with her high color, Hetty was bound to soon develop fat ankles, so therefore Araminta had made it her mission to match Hetty with a worthy contender "before it was too late".

Meanwhile Stephen was warming to his theme as he procured a glass of champagne from the tray of a passing waiter for himself, and orgeat for Hetty. "A traitor risks the gallows. Since our last conversation I've heard even more alarming stories."

"So Sir Aubrey would slit my throat if he regarded me as a threat?" Hetty knew she sounded combative.

"Really, Hetty, now you're being childish." Cousin Stephen squeezed her arm in a brotherly fashion. "Lord Debenham has made these claims and Lord Debenham is a highly regarded politician. Sir Aubrey, by contrast, is a wastrel. He sought public office but no one would sponsor him. The reasons speak for themselves."

"Lord Debenham?" Araminta joined the conversation, adding in eager tones, "There he is dancing with Miss Pangbourne. I expect he'll ask me for one of the next, don't you think?"

"I'm sure he will if that's what you desire." Stephen quirked an eyebrow. "And you'd do well to snare him, though I've heard tell he has something of a reputation for playing fast and loose with feminine hearts."

"Oh yes, he was madly in love with his cousin Lady Margaret, who killed herself last year." Araminta tapped Hetty on the shoulder with her fan as she said in knowledgeable tones, "Lady Margaret was married to Sir Aubrey but Cousin Stephen warns we must steer clear of Sir Aubrey. Not that it's a concern for you, Hetty, however I really don't know what I'll say to put him off when he comes across and asks me to dance."

"I dare you to refuse," Hetty challenged. "Oh look, Lord Debenham *is* looking at you, Araminta. And I think his *is* coming over here."

Hetty closed her gaping mouth as she stared at the raven-haired gentleman whose severe black dress was alleviated by a snowy-white cravat. He looked the height of sartorial elegance, yet there was something sinister and unnerving about his arrogant bearing and the almost disdainful way he looked down his Roman nose at Araminta, whom he had clearly in his sights.

As he engaged her sister to dance, Hetty decided that a man who wore shirt points sharp enough to cut one's throat, and whose shoes, like his hair, were polished to the gleam of a raven's wing, was not to be trusted.

"So you'd approve of a match between Araminta and Lord Debenham?" Hetty asked, as Stephen led her onto the dance floor for the following dance.

"I think there are more amenable partners than Lord Debenham but Araminta would be anyone's match."

Discovering she'd mistaken the sequence of her dance steps, Hetty was relieved when Stephen seized her to polka down the center of the two rows of couples. However, her relief turned to disgust in the middle of her next dance with Cousin Stephen when she saw Sir Aubrey lingering near the entrance to the ballroom, an expression of rapt interest upon his face. For the person who was holding him in such thrall was none other than Araminta, looking more than ever like Sarafina the family cat. As the couple broke apart, Sir Aubrey bowed to Araminta whom he must have waylaid immediately after her dance with Lord Debenham. Then, after another gallant bow, he took his leave through the double doors, quitting the ballroom.

Hetty wasn't sure if it was better to be deprived of at least the presence of the most enticing guest, or if she should be relieved not to have to watch him making up to her sister all night. Nevertheless, it made for a gloomy couple of hours as she alternatively sat out the many dances where she was overlooked by the various eager young blades or jaded gentlemen here tonight, or was partnered by kind Cousin Stephen.

"Smile, Hetty. Please do," he now exhorted her. "You have such lovely dimples and such a pretty smile but I'd wager I'm the only one here tonight who knows it."

Hetty was just about to respond that he probably would only ever be the one to know it because there may never yet be anything to smile about again when a missed dance step at the end of their set caused her to squeal in dismay as she trod upon the hem of her dress. Clutching at the skirt, which had partly separated from the bodice, she sent her cousin a stricken look. "Look what I've done! And here's Mr. Woking, the only other person who's ever asked me to dance, coming to claim me for the quadrille. Oh, do come up with an excuse, Cousin Stephen, for I'll be tongue-tied with embarrassment at having to explain what I don't know how to put into words."

Stephen smiled. "Poor Hetty, why, I'll tell him the truth, of course—that you must make a dash to the ladies' mending room. I hope the damage is not too severe."

"I think I'd rather spend the rest of the evening closeted in the antechambers where things are a little less exciting than here, where I'm out of my depth," she muttered as she took her leave.

* * *

Hetty had spoken only the truth, she decided when she was safely ensconced in a small room where she was attended to by a hunchbacked seamstress. The only other occupant was a young lady who lay facedown, sobbing on the chaise longue by the window.

"That's Miss Hoskings. Bin there all night," the old crone informed her when Hetty's concern failed to elicit a response from the distraught young lady. "'Parently the gennelmun what she thought was goin' to marry her has been makin' up to another young lady."

The girl gave a choking sob and half rose, before throwing herself back down upon the upholstery, wailing, "He's still going to make me an offer and it's not because he cares for me." She wiped her face with the back of her hand as she sat up and glared at Hetty, adding, "And I'm going to accept him though Mama says I could do better."

Hetty took in the girl's narrow shoulders and bad skin and felt sorry for her. Fortunately Hetty's skin was a glowing advertisement of her robust good health. Her once over-generous proportions, too, had diminished to the extent that, though still plump, she'd had several gowns taken in during the past several weeks. Darling Mama had said that she'd been just the same when she'd been Hetty's age and was far comelier after a couple years of marriage than she had been when she was a debutante.

Bolsteringly, Hetty said, "Maybe you could wait a little. I, too, expect to have an offer before the end of the season, for Papa has been generous with my dowry." She suspected it was the chief reason for Mr. Woking's interest and the thought gave her no

15

pleasure. "Though I don't want to marry a man who's only interested in my money."

"Better that than be an ape-leader. What could be worse than being an old maid for the rest of my life?" Miss Hoskings asked gloomily after several loud sniffs. With her red nose and blotchy skin, Hetty feared that was a very likely fate and not one she wished for herself under any circumstances. With another resounding sigh, Miss Hoskings, who was clearly not in a mood to be comforted, went on, "This is my second season and I have three sisters. If I don't marry soon, do you know how I'll spend the rest of my days? Tending Papa's gouty foot, dancing attendance upon my irascible grandmother and looking after everyone else's needs but my own. Well, I won't do it. I've seen the thankless existence my maiden aunts have endured and being an unpaid companion is not for me. Better a loveless marriage, I say!"

Hetty considered their respective situations and wondered if desperation would one day send her down the aisle with a man who cared only for her money and not a jot for her.

Miss Hoskings, who declared she was not going to emerge from the mending room until the night was over, bade Hetty a gloomy farewell once Hetty's skirt was mended but Hetty wasn't sure she felt like reentering the ballroom either. The only person of any interest had left and she had no wish to endure Araminta's preening self- satisfaction as she recounted her success with Sir Aubrey who, if he really were such a dangerous man, would consequently be of even greater interest to her sister, she supposed. No, Hetty had no chance.

"Make sure you turn the right way. The 'ouse is a fair rabbit warren of rooms and yer don't want to end up in the gennulmen's quarters that way." The old crone stabbed a finger up the stairs to the left. "Even that Sir Aubrey what's staying 'ere got hisself lost. Put 'is head in 'ere just afore you came to inquire as to which way was the lobby so he could order hisself a carriage."

Miss Hoskings straightened, her look suddenly interested. "Sir Aubrey is a houseguest, I believe," she said with a sharp look at Hetty. "Handsome gentleman, don't you think? And with that unusual hair."

Just the mere mention of him made Hetty's heart leap. So Sir Aubrey's room was just down the passage and up the stairs? She hesitated as the old seamstress closed the door behind her, plunging her into the gloom of the dimly lit corridor.

The stairs beckoned a short distance away.

What would be the harm in a quick look? No one would see her and she could always claim she'd lost her way. She'd be believed and besides, all the chambers would be empty since everyone was at the ball. The night was still young and no one would be returning yet.

Hetty, curious by nature, found this too tantalizing an opportunity to resist. With a furtive look around her, she hurried left and up the stairs, at which point two corridors at right angles disappeared into darkness. Choosing the one to the right, she found herself face-to-face with a series of closed doors.

Foolish, she chided herself. Of course they were closed and she could hardly open them. As she turned back toward the ballroom, a faint light shining from the crack beneath a door that was slightly ajar gleamed beckoningly.

With a furtive look over her shoulder, she approached it, and when she gave the door a little nudge with her foot, it swung open.

Excitement rippled through her.

"Hello?" she asked in a low voice. She took another step into the room. "Is anyone in here?"

Silence. A low fire burned in the grate before which was a table, against which were propped several items, including a familiar silver-topped cane. Her breath caught. The last time she'd seen that cane was when Sir Aubrey had exchanged several words with Araminta in the street as Hetty had been bringing up the rear with Mrs. Monks. Of course Sir Aubrey had not looked twice at her, excusing himself before having to be introduced to the younger sister and the chaperone who'd nearly closed the gap.

Heart hammering, Hetty closed the door behind her and went to pick up the cane. How fortunate to have stumbled into Sir Aubrey's room, she thought when she observed the fine coat lying upon the bed, apparently discarded in favor of what he was wearing tonight.

He really was a nonpareil, wearing his clothes as if they were an extension of his athletic physique.

Yet he was dangerous, she had to remind herself. Meaning she should not be here, which of course she shouldn't, regardless of whether he was dangerous or not.

But how such a scion of good breeding and genteel society

could be guilty of such a heinous crime as treason, Hetty could not imagine. And surely the story of the runaway wife was a gilded one. It was all the stuff of make-believe and Cousin Stephen was only telling Hetty he was dangerous to curb her schoolroom daydreams.

Turning, she saw half protruding from beneath the suit of clothes what appeared to be the edge of a silver, filigreed box. It was partly obscured by the overhang of the counterpane, as if it hadn't properly been returned to its hiding place.

A moment's indecision made her pause but soon Hetty was crouching on the floor, closing clammy fingers around the box. Might it contain secrets? Ones that would reveal, conclusively, what Cousin Stephen claimed was true?

Alternatively, proof that would exonerate Sir Aubrey?

Hetty fumbled for the catch. Dear Lord, this was too exciting for words. Perhaps Sir Aubrey was a secret agent working for the English, and Stephen had no idea.

Perhaps he was—

Protesting door hinges made her gasp as the door was flung wide. Hetty let the lid of the box fall and retreated into the shadows as Sir Aubrey strode into the room.

He was breathing heavily as he shrugged off his jacket with a curse, raindrops spattering into the hissing fire as he raked his fingers through his hair. A curious stillness overtook him and he froze, obviously sensing all was not as he left it.

He sniffed the air. "Orange flower water," he muttered, stepping closer to the fire, fumbling for the tinderbox on the mantelpiece to light another candle.

Immediately he was thrown into sharp relief and as he stared at Hetty, it was not his look of shock and suspicion that made her scream—but the copious amounts of blood that stained his shirtsleeves and once-snowy linen cravat.

"God Almighty, who are you?" he demanded as his gaze raked her finery. "You're no parlor maid, that's for certain."

Gaping, unable to formulate a sensible answer, Hetty finally managed, "What happened to your arm, Sir Aubrey? Are you injured?"

"Sir Aubrey, is it? So you know who I am!" He grunted as he looked down at his arm, the bloodied linen shredded over the long graze. "It's not as bad as it looks and I assure you, I gave a good account of myself." His laugh was more a sneer. "Indeed, my assailant lies dead in the gutter."

Hetty gasped. "Dueling?" Myriad questions crowded her mind. Could this be to do with Araminta? Had Sir Aubrey left Araminta in the middle of the ball to fight some other contender for her affections?

"Dueling?" he repeated. He shook his head and Hetty drew back at the coldness in his eyes. "There was nothing noble about my activities this evening. I was set upon in a dark alley. A short scuffle ensued, I drew my knife, then…" With his hand, he made a gesture like the slitting of his throat, adding, "I am slightly wounded but as I said, my attacker does not live to repeat the insult."

Her horror clearly amused him, for his eyes narrowed while his generous mouth quirked. He looked like an incarnation of the most handsome demon she'd ever seen depicted in the fairy stories she loved to read.

"We all have enemies, madam. Enemies who must be eliminated if we are to breathe freely."

Chapter Three

AUBREY WAS ENJOYING the girl's wide-eyed terror. No doubt she imagined he'd sliced the throat of a footpad, not the snarling, mangy cur who had leapt upon him as he'd been returning from his brief assignation to settle a gaming debt incurred by his favorite reprobate nephew.

Taking pity on her, he said reassuringly, "Don't worry. I won't hurt you." Her fearful look as he removed first his jacket, then the bloodied shirt he tossed upon the bed before he rose to his full height, bare chested, afforded him the most amusement he'd had in a long time. "So, you're the girl Maggie Montgomery sent?"

She simply stared at him and he nodded appraisingly as he sat on the bed and pulled off his boots. "You had me fooled for a moment. I thought you really were some innocent who'd lost her way in these catacombs." Had he not been so jaded he might have been ashamed at the assessment in his tone when he added, "My faithful procuress threatened to one day surprise me—and that I'd not be able to tell the difference." He chuckled and put out his hand. Actually, he had very little regard for Maggie Montgomery but since the young girl before him had obviously chosen to work for the notorious brothel madam he considered it gentlemanly to say something generous to allay any fears she might have, considering the fact she was looking distinctly nervous. "Well, come into the light so I can see you better. After the god-awful night I've had, you might be just what I need: the retiring sort—for I'm sick to death of women who like to play games."

Like that Miss Araminta Partington, he thought. Now didn't she like to play games, with her speaking looks and half-whispered promises? Which wasn't to say he hadn't enjoyed his brief assignation with her in an antechamber behind the supper room.

He'd been on his way out to settle his nephew's wager when Miss Partington had waylaid him before proving extremely amenable to a kiss and a fondle. But of course that was as far as it could go and his throbbing groin after that little encounter had been one good reason to slip unnoticed out of Lady Knox's townhouse.

Unsatisfied desire had made him restless for the rest of the night. He certainly didn't want Miss Araminta Partington as his wife but she'd appeared very amenable to going further than the usual debutante. And while Aubrey was the first to know this was very dangerous territory, the surfeit of promise and lack of action had put him in a particularly unsatisfied mood.

Aubrey smiled at the girl. He could tell she was new to the game, though Aubrey was not a frequent visitor to Maggie Montgomery's elegant Soho premises. However, after being dragged there one night by a friend when he was in the latter stages of grief over his wife's death, he had formed a rather intense liaison with a flaming redhead called Jezebel.

After Jezebel had transferred her affections to an ageing baronet, Aubrey had ceased his visits until he'd found himself in Maggie's plush parlor one night with several similarly drunken associates.

It was when he'd declined the delights Maggie's girls could offer him, that Maggie had made her wager.

Now, it appeared, she'd finally followed through.

And Aubrey, who had always been rather repelled by the thought of paying for sex, now found himself in a curious situation.

The young lady's contrived innocence was having a strange effect upon him. It would seem Maggie Montgomery had read him correctly, for even he hadn't realized how tired he was of worldly sophistication.

"Yes, sit here." He patted his knees. "No need to carry the pretense to quite such extremes. That's right. I want you to sit on my lap so I can…observe you better."

"Sit on your lap?" she squeaked as he tugged at her hand and her rounded bottom landed on his thighs.

He ran his hands over her contours appreciatively. She was rather a nice little thing with a familiarity that tugged at his memory. Plump and almost pretty, though he rather fancied she had the makings of a beauty. Not that her future development was of concern since he had her only for one night. Maggie would have sent her on approval. Indeed, she did seem vaguely familiar. It was quite possible he'd seen the chit at the brothel and unconsciously dismissed her on account of the very reasons Maggie had sent her—for her innocence and youth.

He ran his fingers through her fine light-brown curls and contoured her neck appreciatively, amused that she tensed as if this had never happened to her before. Well, if he liked her, he'd see her as often as he wished over the following month. By the time the abbess presented him with one of her exorbitant accounts, he'd know whether the girl gave value enough to continue the arrangement.

If she pleased him as much as his former mistress Jezebel had, Aubrey would indeed be seeing more of her. The next hour or so would tell.

"Oh sir!" she cried, jumping up as his hand came into contact with her breast. "What are you doing?"

He grinned as he tugged her back down and resettled her across his knees. "Maggie Montgomery has trained you well. Now I suppose you'll tell me you're a virgin."

She nodded vigorously. "I am, sir. Indeed I am and—"

His scowl made her stiffen with apparent terror. Oh, she was good.

"Really?" He reached for the cutlass that had fallen from his belt and now lay at his feet. Idly he stroked the blade, stained with the dead dog's blood, while he contemplated her. She was indulging in the charade perhaps a little too enthusiastically but then, as he narrowed his gaze and saw how frightened she really seemed, it occurred to him that he was moving too quickly. Every whore would remember her 'first time' and the customer who had broken her in. If this girl had never done this before, of course she'd be terrified.

He was a trifle irritated with Maggie. She knew he would never have accepted the services of a virgin but clearly she'd decided to play her little trick on him tonight.

During his last visit, she'd told him he needed softening. That the effects of the opprobrium directed at him since poor Margaret's death had stripped him of his humanity.

He frowned into the large, soft brown eyes of the girl on his lap and felt a tug of humanity. Yes, definitely *humanity*. Perhaps tonight was the time to start cultivating his more tender side, after all.

"A virgin?" Before, he would have spoken with blatant skepticism. Now he would allow that she could be telling the truth.

She nodded, her eyes riveted on the blade he was now using to clean his fingernails. "So this will be your first time with a man?"

She drew in a trembling breath and repeated stupidly, "First time with a man?"

He tried not to sound irritated. There was only so much of the playacting he could take. "Mrs Montgomery obviously selected you on account of your innocence. She knows my proclivities and that experience is my preference but I can be gentle. I won't hurt you." He grinned as he was struck by the responsibility of breaking in a virgin. One who would always remember her first time with him, no matter how many paying customers she serviced in her working life.

He put down his knife and licked his lips as he watched understanding dawn, adding as he traced the edge of her décolletage with his right forefinger, "In fact, I promise that you'll quite enjoy the experience. God knows, you're going to endure enough during your career, so you might as well start off on a good note. Now, shall we begin?"

"Oh sir, I don't know what to do!" She twisted in his lap and stared frantically at the door.

Chuckling, he whisked her into his arms and tossed her, not roughly, onto the bed, caging her body with his and staring down into her frightened face.

"Oh, I can help you there. I promise." He touched her nose with his forefinger. "You really are a rather engaging little thing. But of course, if you've changed your mind and want to leave, I shan't deny you that option."

Poor child, he thought, wondering briefly what had brought her to this when she shook her head and made no move to leave.

Well, she'd clearly chosen this life in preference to honest toil, and she was lucky her procuress hadn't given her to any number of brutes he knew of who would initiate her in far less gentle fashion than he intended.

In what he hoped was a sufficiently reassuring tone, he murmured, "So, you're happy to stay here in my arms while I show you just how much pleasure can be enjoyed by both parties? Good. Now, just lie back. I promise I won't hurt you."

She bit her lip, nodding, her wide-eyed—he'd go so far as to say *excited* gaze—following his hand, which reached down to grasp the hem of her gown.

Maggie Montgomery spared no expense on her girls and this one was dressed in finery to equal that of any daughter of the peerage. No doubt she'd been taught to speak like a duke's daughter. And to behave with fitting grace and decorum if required. Aubrey recalled with amusement the occasion he'd taken Jezebel— renamed Lady Anne for the occasion—to visit his mother when the dowager had been hell-bent on allying Aubrey with some horsey-looking cousin, saying his twelve-month mourning period was over and it was hardly as though Margaret had been a good wife. That the time had come to sire an heir.

Jezebel, though she'd been born in the gutter, had given as good an account of herself as any peeress.

He sent the girl beneath him another appreciative glance. He needed diversion and a pair of arms to sink into. Someone who'd at least pretend softness and comfort at the end of a difficult day. A difficult day? Every day was a battle. Almost convulsively his mind was drawn back to the difficulties pressing upon him with regard to his blackened reputation, before he returned his concentration to the task at hand, and his hand to the girl's warm, soft thighs, which yielded at his gentle pressure to part them.

"That's right," he murmured. "Slow and steady. Just let your knees go slack and I'll start off doing what's required to break you in, my sweetheart, just like I promised. I want you to give a good report of me to your madam when you return."

"Sir, I—"

But when ran his fingers gently over her mound, she jerked into awareness and her words died on her lips. She was damp but not wet as she needed to be when he breached her defenses, so to speak.

Ah well, it was no hardship to have to work harder. Maggie no doubt would charge like a wounded bull and, given a choice, he'd have roundly rejected the idea of enjoying the services of a *virgin*, but he was feeling strangely attracted to the lass he'd been sent.

Lowering his head, he gently touched his lips to hers, tracing her upper lip with the tip of his tongue before breaching the seam, gently breaking the seal of her teeth so he could explore her sweet mouth.

He was surprised by her drawn-out sigh and the way her body went slack so quickly. As if she truly relished the kiss. He was surprised, too, by the extent to which he was affected. He drew back to study her more closely.

She couldn't have been more than eighteen. So young, but the age at which respectable girls were married off. Had she been born into more fortunate circumstances she would be mixing with the throng downstairs, not closeted in a gentleman's bedroom learning how to pleasure a whole lineup of them.

The poor child was destined for a hard life but the least he could do in exchange for taking her virginity was to show her what she should demand from all future liaisons: respect and pleasure. He'd only broken in one virgin, his beautiful wife Margaret, and she, who'd been terrified, had come to relish the act. Well, until that bastard Debenham, as he now was, had returned to haunt her. Sir Aubrey forced the thought from his mind. It would drive him mad if he let it.

He licked his finger before finding the swollen nub between her legs, massaging her rhythmically, gently, in her most intimate parts, enjoying her sudden breathlessness and the changes in the feel of her body. She was growing wetter by the minute.

"Oh…my lord," she breathed, gripping him more tightly.

It was nice to feel in charge of a woman's pleasure once more. By the end of his liaison with Jezebel, the attainment of sexual gratification had become an unspoken contest between them as they'd writhed, panting, almost combative, in one another's arms.

"Oh!" She jerked when he slowly pushed a finger inside her, preparing her. He could almost imagine she'd never even touched herself before, her reaction was so genuinely startled.

"You like it?" he asked in a low growl as he rucked her skirt up over her hips using one hand before attending to his own buttons with his usual speed and efficiency. He was a man of strong sexual impulses and part of the game Jezebel had played with him was to appear when he'd least expected it. As if she—or perhaps Maggie— had access to his private diary. Once, Aubrey had paid his great-aunt a visit at the convent in Lincoln where she'd offered her devotions for the previous fifty years. As he was leaving, he'd been accosted by a nun and drawn into the shrubbery behind the high walls. It had been Jezebel, let loose from one priory, so to speak, to seek him out in another for some fast and furious rutting. Highly irreverent, of course, and all the more entertaining for the fact.

Now this little creature was all his for the breaking in and his ministrations would stay with her for the rest of her life.

"Just lie back and enjoy it. I said I wouldn't hurt you." The roughness of his voice and his deep scowl were a cover for a sudden concern completely out of character. Whores were for pleasuring him. They did it for financial gain. He was an experienced lover, he did not engage in gross and violent acts, and beyond that their feelings were of no account. Well, that's what he'd always told himself so he was irritated by the softening of his attitude towards this little one. He liked to think he was immune to sentiment.

Still, he was amused by her obvious shock and stifled gasp when he tossed off his breeches and his member sprang free.

"More than you were expecting, sweetheart?" He chuckled as he rolled her onto her stomach and quickly undid the buttons on the back of her dress. "Let's remove this, shall we? Mrs Montgomery will not thank me for spoiling her wares—though I pay her well enough for the privilege." As he hauled her up beneath her arms into a sitting position, he reconsidered his strategy.

"Sit on the edge of the bed," he told her as he stood. "That's right. Now grasp me. That's right. Never felt a man's member before? Well, you're in for a treat." He shuddered, closing his eyes in rapture as her little hands closed around him. This was just what he needed after the evening he'd had. A sweet, pliant creature he could tutor and whose inexperience required him to be gentle.

"Now stand up, turn around and put out your hands to support yourself on the bed. I'm going to enter you from behind, but from this angle I can pleasure you until you are screaming with desire. Believe me, you'll feel nothing but a burst of rapture as we do the deed." He chuckled again. "I hope that was a gasp of anticipation."

He leaned over her, covering her small body with his large one, reaching around so he could continue to fondle her. Her short, jerky movements indicated her growing excitement and it pleased him. Her thighs and lovely rounded bottom were moist with sweat as her breathing escalated. Meanwhile he curbed his own desire to thrust into her. He had to time this just right. She was tensing, releasing, tensing, even though she'd obviously never done this before, playing the game like the pro she was on the way to becoming and he was enjoying it as much as she.

When he felt her suck in her breath and hold it, as if she balanced on the edge of the precipice and didn't know what else to do, he entered her gently, increasing the rhythmic pressure of his fingers upon the swollen nub nestled within the folds of her sex. With a gasp, she bucked against him, crying out as she reared again and again, her unbridled pleasure igniting his own so that his climax occurred shortly afterward.

Instantly he withdrew, spilling his seed, which trickled down his leg. With a rapidly beating heart, he held her close to his chest, idly toying with her soft, full breasts beneath her chemise before he scooped her up and tossed her onto the bed, crawling up beside her.

"That wasn't too bad, was it?" he asked, tucking her beneath the covers and cradling her head on his chest. The intimacy was surprisingly enjoyable. "I'm sure Mrs Montgomery reassured you that you'd be in expert hands. There are plenty of other ways we can do this and you gave every indication you're eager to learn more."

He glanced over at her. She looked dazed but not terrified as she had earlier. "You don't talk much, do you?"

She swallowed and her voice was faint. "I don't really know what to say, sir?"

"Well, I didn't like the idea before but enjoying the exclusive services of the virgin I broke in has its benefits. For one thing I needn't worry about the pox, eh?" He chuckled. "No cundums, though of course there's still the need for coitus interruptus. I'll not foist a brat on you. Only my wife will have my children."

He pulled her even closer against him. She was a nicely rounded little thing and he felt protective of her in a way he had not with Jezebel or the few other experienced mistresses he'd had in his lifetime.

"So…you do not have a wife?" She appeared to be gaining assurance.

"I did…once." God, but the memory still tore at him. He stared at the ceiling. "A dear, sweet creature when I married her—until she was enticed into the arms of another." He gave a harsh laugh at her murmured commiserations. "In the eighteen months since I've lost her I've more than compensated, though in truth, no rutting has come close to what I experienced in the arms of my dear Margaret. I'm a sentimental fool at heart."

She swallowed, audibly. "I heard you're a dangerous man. Not a sentimental fool, sir."

"A dangerous man," he repeated, wishing he didn't feel such an impotent one when it came to rejuvenating his unfairly tarnished reputation. His nemesis, Debenham—his wife's cousin and lover and the man who was working hard to destroy him—had friends in high places. "No, lass, I'm a man with enemies but I am on a mission to clear my name. Mark my words, I shall bring to justice the one who is intent on ruining me."

Her mouth dropped open. "Who, sir?"

He considered her a moment. In the dim light her eyes were luminous and her question seemed innocent enough.

"A man called Debenham. My late wife's cousin, in fact. He claims he has proof that I'm a felon. A letter found clutched in the hand of my darling Margaret when she died purports to the fact...*apparently*." He made sure she registered his irony. "Conveniently, it has now gone missing."

She raised herself onto her elbows, her look haunted. "So you are *not* a dangerous man?"

"I'm sure there are those who might consider me so—namely Debenham if I'm able to find proof that the boot's on the other foot and that he's the traitor in their midst." He sat up and chucked her under the chin. "And now it is time for me to cast you out, for I have work to do, though I'll render you the small service of fastening your dress once you've availed yourself of my washbasin."

When he'd finished working on her buttons, he raked her with his appreciative gaze. "My, but a good tupping has done you the world of good. Your color and the brightness of your eyes are much improved. Pray inform Mrs Montgomery that I will require your exclusive services for at least the next month. No doubt her account will be exorbitant."

* * *

Dazed, Hetty trailed through the corridors of Lady Knox's residence until the strains of the music drew her toward the ballroom.

"There you are!" Araminta pounced as Hetty hesitated on the

threshold. Her sister gripped her wrist and hauled her roughly into the room. "I've been looking all over for you. No doubt you've been cowering in the mending room, too afraid a man will look at you and you won't know what to do. Well, Hetty, you're just going to have to gain more experience in order to make a gentleman want to pass the time in your company with idle small talk, much less do anything else. Mr. Woking was asking for you, and although I know he's not much to look at, beggars can't be choosers."

"I'm not a beggar."

"No, you have something in the way of a dowry but then so do many other girls, including me...girls far comelier, meaning you'll just have to take what you can get. Ah, there he is!"

Araminta raised her arm to hail someone across the room as Hetty asked, "Who?"

"Mr. Woking, of course. He wants to dance with you and you could do worse to court his interest."

"But he's got spots and terrible breath. *You* wouldn't want to dance with him, would you?"

"Of course not. I've got my sights set on someone far more my equal."

"Lord Debenham?"

Araminta looked uncomfortable. "I learned a few things about Lord Debenham tonight that make me think Sir Aubrey is the better candidate." Then she simpered, adding in a furtive whisper, "He has made his interest very clear and I mean to see that it goes somewhere."

Hetty's insides cleaved. "Sir Aubrey has?" Her legs felt shaky and she had no idea whether she was going to laugh or cry. "Cousin Stephen says he's not a friend of England." She didn't know what to make of this statement now, not after what Sir Aubrey had told her about his quarrel with Lord Debenham. She'd only succumbed to his advances through her fear that he was capable of murder.

She caught herself up as, in the aftermath of shock, she questioned her true motives.

If she'd truly only succumbed to his advances through terror, why, then, had she stayed when he'd given her the opportunity to leave?

She closed her eyes briefly as she recalled everything that had just happened.

When Sir Aubrey had walked into his bedchamber and

discovered Hetty in the shadows, he'd been covered with blood. He'd admitted just killing a man. Then he'd all but ordered her to submit as he'd toyed with the blade of his cutlass. What choice had she had?

A frisson of discomfort ran up her spine as she answered the question. She *had* had a choice. He'd said she could leave but she'd just stayed right where she was, staring up into the face of the only man who had made her heart thump with excited anticipation…as he explained exactly how he was going to make love to her.

Yet, overwhelming though the experience was, she felt— instead of ashamed and horrified—exhilarated. Sir Aubrey had evoked glorious sensations within her. She'd not known it was possible to feel like that. And he, a man who was supposedly a fiend, had been responsible. Well, he *wasn't* a fiend. His reputation had been falsely tarnished by none other than Lord Debenham.

Araminta tossed her head. "Cousin Stephen has served in the Foreign Office less than a month. What does he know? Ah, Mr. Woking, here is my sister and she tells me she's simply dying for the pleasure of partnering you."

In a haze of confusion and mixed emotions, Hetty went through her dance steps with the stoop-shouldered young man who was clearly at pains to engage her interest by the enthusiasm with which he told her of his expectations.

All Hetty could think of was the rampant endowments of her erstwhile lover and wonder why she was not feeling ruined and violated. She'd never kissed a man before tonight. Heavens, she'd never done anything remotely exciting with a man until tonight. She should be horrified with herself, yet after her initial fear, she'd relished every second.

She lowered her eyes. It would be her secret. She'd carry it to her grave—her one moment of wild abandon. For once, she'd have something over Araminta.

Mr. Woking was speaking to her. She plastered on an attentive smile as she asked him to repeat himself.

"That's my uncle over there. He's the member of parliament for Westhaven." He looked proud.

Hetty glanced in the direction Mr. Woking was pointing and choked on a gasp. "Lord Debenham is your *uncle*?"

Several gentlemen had their heads bent in earnest discussion. The taller one, with the jet-black locks and the dangerous glint in his eye, surely did not hail from the same planet as Mr. Woking.

"You don't look anything like him." The words were out before she could check herself.

Sadly, Mr. Woking did not favor his uncle. Even at his young age his hair was rapidly thinning. His nervous habit of glancing around jerkily, rather like a bird pecking at crumbs, was as far removed from Lord Debenham's sartorial elegance as Hetty could imagine.

Mr. Woking cleared his throat. "He's a step-uncle, actually. The brother of my father's third wife."

"Your father married three times?" Again Hetty failed to filter her thoughts. Surely he must guess that her surprise did not stem from anything to flatter his father.

The jerky way Mr. Woking rearranged his body at her remark made Hetty think a poker had been rammed up his bottom, though the look in his eye suggested prickly pride. "Lord Debenham is working to rid this country of traitors. Traitors like the Spenceans." He brought his face closer to Hetty's, as if he were searching for something, and she forced herself not to recoil from his unpleasant breath. When he straightened, the glint in his eye suggested she'd passed some test. "Have you heard of Sir Aubrey?"

He lowered his voice, apparently not registering Hetty's sudden rigidity or no doubt, look of horror. "Perhaps your sister has said something, for I have been watching Sir Aubrey closely and it would appear he is most interested in Miss Partington."

Hetty stumbled in his embrace and he caught her close— too close and for too long—before she pushed him back, saying proudly, "I think you are mistaken. I've noticed nothing."

"You'd do well to warn her to take care, Miss Henrietta. Sir Aubrey is my uncle's quarry. I reveal nothing that the villainous Sir Aubrey doesn't already know. However you seem a good, trustworthy sort, and so I am entrusting you with this secret."

"In order to keep Araminta safe?" She rather suspected something deeper was at play here.

"That," he paused, "and to help deliver justice. Perhaps you'd care to inform me if you notice anything untoward."

"Like what?"

He shrugged. Perhaps he didn't know. He was trying to impress her. She'd not believe it.

Smugly he announced, "Sir Aubrey is a Spencean. A man

who plots with the enemy to overturn society and plunge us into revolution like the French. He was involved in the attempted assassination of Lord Castlereagh."

Hetty shook her head. Clearly he interpreted this as shock rather than denial for he went on, his tone intimate, "His late wife had evidence that has gone missing, for indeed it was my uncle who saw the incriminating letter with his own eyes. It is his mission to find that letter so that justice will be served and Sir Aubrey and his like no longer threaten the values we uphold."

Hetty realized she was gaping like a fish. In less than an hour she'd been given two wildly varying stories. She knew who she wanted to believe but...

"Miss Henrietta, I would ask you to keep your ears and eyes open. If your sister reveals anything to you—"

The music faded away and Hetty broke apart to see Araminta coming toward her, Cousin Stephen in her wake. She wondered if Mr. Woking and Cousin Stephen had shared their concerns.

"It's time to go home, Hetty." Araminta patted her sister's shoulder condescendingly. "You're only just out and you're not used to such excitement."

Excitement? Hetty wondered if she'd ever enjoy such excitement again and wished she felt more filled with shame.

Confusion, fear and doubt, she felt in abundance. But not shame over what she'd done tonight. All the could recall was the kindness, consideration and passion Sir Aubrey had displayed towards her in equal measure.

Hetty had always been easily shamed by actions that displayed disobedience or willfulness, in the eyes of her governess, but for some strange reason she felt no shame at what she'd done tonight.

Perhaps that would come, though she didn't think so.

She exhaled on a sigh of contented rapture. Everything she and Sir Aubrey had done had felt so right.

Chapter Four

IT WAS A beautiful evening for a night of revelry at Vauxhall Gardens, warm and sultry, with a blaze of stars just starting to twinkle in the twilight.

Although Araminta had declared that Hetty would benefit from an early night "so the shadows under her eyes might be less in evidence" and "in the hope that her skin might look brighter", as she told Cousin Stephen, her loyal cousin had gallantly responded by saying Hetty was on the way to becoming a beauty like their mother. He didn't say she already was, but it was sufficient to bolster her spirits so that seeing her sister's nose put out of joint was almost as enjoyable as being made a party to such an exciting event, albeit one that included their deadly dull cousins Seb, who was in the army, and his two turkey-necked sisters, Mary and Amelia. They were distant family members from the country and, as their dress and manner immediately proclaimed them country bumpkins, they were of complete disinterest to Araminta who barely concealed her distaste at being forced to entertain them.

Hetty was not surprised when Araminta seized upon the first opportunity to separate from them. The crowd was now a roiling mass of humanity within the hub of the gardens. Hetty had visited Vauxhall before and was familiar with the layout but the crowds were disconcerting. It would be easy to become lost.

Peering past a floral-festooned headdress, Araminta cried out in feigned surprise, "Oh goodness, Cousin Stephen, why, isn't that Miss Cordelia Entwistle and her brother? Don't you remember what a jolly time we had together playing charades at Lady Wainright's house party last summer?" With a falsely pitying smile, she grasped Cousin Seb's wrist, murmuring, "They lost their dear brother at Waterloo. Anything to remind them of the army sends poor Miss Cordelia in paroxysms of grief. Perhaps it's best if you didn't accompany us to offer our greetings, for they have seen us in the crowd and we must go to them." Already she was moving on, her grip now transferred to Cousin Stephen's wrist as she said over her shoulder, "I propose we meet in an hour in the supper room we've bespoken in the Druid's Walk."

Hetty started to follow, stopping with dismay as her sister called across the lengthening distance that now separated them, "Hetty, you must keep company with Cousins Amelia and Mary. They can chaperone you until we meet again."

Grumbling, Hetty turned. Her cousins were a lackluster trio. Yet when none of them could be seen amidst the roiling throng, their company was suddenly never more desirable. Especially when, dashing after Araminta, Hetty discovered that every single member of her original party appeared to have vanished into thin air.

Breathless, she came to a junction of pathways, her terror increasing when she still could see no sign of them. What if she was observed, alone? Her reputation would be in tatters.

"Mayhap sweet Cupid pursues me once more?"

Hetty swung 'round at the sound of the familiar low growl, gasping as she found herself staring into the handsome face of...well, the man who'd seduced her only days before. "Sir Aubrey!"

He flashed her a sardonic smile as he clapped her on the shoulder. It was such a familiar gesture from a gentleman...

And yet not nearly as familiar as they'd enjoyed. And while she'd relished every single moment, it had been so wrong. Of her, Hetty. She'd led him to believe something that wasn't true and compromised herself as a result. She'd been as wicked as a young woman could be but she'd got away with her actions. Now if she were discovered alone with Sir Aubrey in such a public place, she'd be ruined. She'd have no choice but to retire quietly to the country, where she'd be destined to live out her days. Survival in every sense depended upon withdrawing into the shadows, evading him so he'd never set eyes upon her again and she could do what she had come to London to do—make a good marriage and start her own independent life.

That would never be possible with Sir Aubrey, she thought with a stab of despair. But, oh, how wonderful it would be if it were!

She contemplated her alternatives while her heart performed

strange contortions in her chest and warm, molten liquid seemed to pool in her lower belly. Her body was betraying her while her mind cried out for reason to prevail.

Perhaps she should simply run. No, that would draw attention to what should not be observed as anything out of the ordinary. She should definitely find some way of slipping out of his grasp and simply disappearing into the crowd. It could be done, yet...

The truth was, there was something so compelling in the weight of his hand and so desirable in the genuine pleasure she saw in his eyes that she was incapable of doing anything other than murmuring, inanely, "What a surprise to see you here, Sir Aubrey."

His grip tightened as he pulled her closer and his soft, appealing voice made her shiver with excitement. "The investigative prowess of your abbess is to be commended. Perhaps I should employ her myself. Come, my angel, I shall spirit you away in my carriage—"

"No, sir...no, I mean, it's not possible right now." The extraordinary thing was that even though Hetty's acquaintance with this man was so limited—and then only to an encounter of the most shocking, carnal kind—she couldn't think of anything more tempting than exploring the other surprises he had to offer in the privacy of his own home.

His expression hardened as he tipped her face up to meet his eye. "Surely you weren't trawling the Serpentine Walk for trade? I thought I'd made it clear—"

"Indeed you did and it's very flattering." Hetty floundered as she searched for a response that would appease him and enable her to retain any shred of respectability. "However, I am on my way to a special event I've promised to attend."

"Special event?"

Wildly, she searched for some plausible excuse. "It's my brother's birthday celebration. I've promised him I'll be there."

"Yet you are here?" He raised an eyebrow, clearly skeptical.

"I am, sir, because...my brother lives not far from here."

"Indeed?" He hesitated, his hand still on her shoulder as he indicated a private supper box secluded by trees at the end of the path they trod. "Surely your brother would not be inconvenienced if you chose to while away half an hour of your time...?" He licked his lips and sent her a look that was both salacious but also filled with genuine desire.

Hetty's stomance curdled with similar desire but she shook her head. "Indeed, I'm expected within half an hour, sir."

"Ten minutes, then!" With clear enthusiasm he ushered her towards the dimly lit supper box. "I can show you how much pleasure there is to be enjoyed in ten short minutes, my dear!"

Longing overlaid with the knowledge that she had to escape made Hetty desperate. More so when Sir Aubrey placed his hands on her shoulders and drew her into his warm embrace after gently pushing her over the threshold and closing the door.

Instant connection vibrated between them. She felt it in his stiffening of awareness, his faint intake of breath.

She could feel his desire pressing against her stomach, unleashing her own rampant need for closer connection. She'd never felt excitement like this yet how, when she knew it was so wrong, could she have found herself in such a situation? Again? What would the repercussions be for her future? For her ability to hold her head high and look her darling mother in the eye?

With a degree of embarrassment, she acknowledged she was more concerned with discovery than the rightness or wrongness of her actual actions.

"The fact that your loyalty to your brother outweighs financial considerations is, I suppose, to be commended." Sir Aubrey's breath caressed her heated ear like a promise as she felt her legs buckle and his arms tighten around her. "Especially when most little ladybirds would be doing all in their power to reel in such a catch as myself."

"It must be a fine thing...to have such a high opinion of oneself, sir," Hetty ventured bravely, trembling as his lips touched hers.

His laugh reverberated gently between them and she opened her eyes to find him shaking his head. "Why, methinks you do not speak in jest. How refreshing." He held her a little tighter before drawing her by the hand to a pile of sumptuous silk cushions in the corner of the room. "And do you have such a high opinion of yourself, my little one? You certainly ought to after the aptitude you showed for one so inexperienced."

"You mean at Lady Knox's ball?"

He folded his lean, muscular frame into a semirecumbent position upon the pillows and pulled Hetty onto his lap. With cocked eyebrow and quirked lips, he regarded her as he might a delectable cream puff. That is, if a man as athletic as Sir Aubrey had a liking for pastries.

"Indeed, at Lady Knox's ball." He gave a short laugh. "When I found you trespassing in my chamber it crossed my mind you were a spy working for Lord Debenham. It was perhaps a dangerous way for your abbess to introduce to me her latest novice. A novelty, certainly, but dangerous. Perhaps I might have slit your throat."

Hetty grimaced. "When I saw you covered with blood, I feared that's what you were about to do, sir. Especially after you confessed you'd just killed a man."

His rumble of laughter brought him into closer proximity. "Lord, did I neglect to tell you the truth? Never mind…" He ran a fingertip from the tip of her nose, tracing her contours until he reached the top of her décolletage. "I've never killed a man and I hope I never do. Ah, but you must be Maggie Montgomery's star creation." He kissed her brow lightly. "Ingenuous, inexperienced and yet you could pass as a lady."

"I could? Well—" His confession that he had in fact never committed murder was decidedly dismaying, removing as it did any acceptable reason for Hetty engaging in the wanton acts she had with the man. Not that she'd truly thought he was a villain but it would have proved a useful reason if her own wickedness ever came to light.

He put his fingertips to her lips. "I do not want to hear your sad and sorry tale. Your acting powers are clearly evident so I'd not believe you, besides which the account I shall receive at the end of the month demanding remuneration for attending to my desires will be a high one, I've no doubt. We both know to what extent business mixes with pleasure in this instance."

There was an edge to his voice, which Hetty found both disturbing and, to her confusion, disappointing. She ought to be glad to have an excuse to revile the man if that's the way he thought; that these carnal activities were no more than a business transaction.

"In that case, sir, I think it must end now, sir." Hetty struggled amidst the cushions into a sitting position. Her smile was regretful as she tried to ignore the fierce disappointement that raged through her.

But he'd given her the excuse to leave that she needed. She was sailing too close to the wind. Amongst a sea of hopeful debutantes, he'd not looked at her twice. If he ever discovered her true identity, he'd be furious! If anyone else discovered, she would be ruined.

"Playing games, are we?" He reached out a languid hand as she rose, not bothering to get up for clearly he did not believe that she intended to leave. "Well, my dear, if you cannot spare the time to attend to me in my own domain, it seems you are in a hurry to expedite proceedings here. I'd thought it a novelty to enjoy some preliminary conversation but if you wish to bypass that, by all means, let us proceed to the carnal part of this evening."

Hetty shook off his hand, incensed by his manner and now more than ready to leave. "I am honored you wish to further our acquaintance," she said with heavy irony. "Indeed, our previous encounter was surprisingly enjoyable but, yes, I really do have to go, I'm afraid."

Clearly he still did not believe her, but as she pulled the door open his eyes widened and he cocked his head.

"Ah, you are adept at this game for one so inexperienced. I think I came to the wrong conclusion earlier. Indeed, you'd prefer to come to me at my townhouse, where you will experience greater comfort and possibly a more rewarding outcome. You want to insinuate yourself more thoroughly into my life. Predictable after all."

Hetty sent him a level stare. "I do not care to visit you in your townhouse when you choose to be so uncivil, sir." She drew back her shoulders, stifling the urge to cry. She'd been wild for this gentleman and yet he *was* indeed the rogue and libertarian he'd been painted. A philanderer with no shred of civility. She inclined her head as she passed through the door. "I'm sorry if I leave you disappointed though I'm certain my shoes will not be too difficult to fill."

His parting words showed he was not the slightest bit shamed. "It was not your shoes I had hoped to fill."

Angrily she slammed the door behind her.

* * *

Sweeping into the night was not the liberating experience she'd expected. For the first time in her life, Hetty realized what it was to be truly alone. She took a couple of tentative steps toward the main walkway, along which small groups and the occasional stray individual meandered, but she lacked the courage to make her isolated state evident, preferring to loiter in the shadows.

What should she do? She couldn't return to Sir Aubrey after what he'd said. She was nothing to him.

For days she'd built up her importance to him through dreams of what might be possible between them when the truth was revealed—at the appropriate time, of course.

Now she knew he must never realize it. The recollection of his voice sent tremors of shame through her. The irony, the entitlement and boredom in his tone revealed him as the kind of man who would consider that she was the one entirely to blame for the loss of her reputation. With a sob, she prepared to sally forth onto the main path but drew back behind the trunk of an elm when she heard male voices, one of which sounded frighteningly familiar. As an unchaperoned debutante she dare not risk exposure.

Hearing the name of her erstwhile…lover…made her hold her breath.

"Sir Aubrey's in there." The faintness of their discussion made it impossible to follow until one of them sniggered, "Entertaining some little ladybird."

The other voice, younger and more serious, interjected softly, "He'll let his guard down one of these days, uncle."

With a start, Hetty realized it was Mr. Woking who spoke with such fawning self- importance. "He will be caught and convicted soon. We cannot afford a repeat of Spa Fields else every landowner will go about in fear of having their throats slit by their laborers." With boyish urgency he added, "But what if we can find no evidence?"

"Then we must weigh up the merits of preserving the peace through resorting to methods whereby evidence is," there was an ominous pause, "discovered."

"But uncle—" Mr. Woking began, however Lord Debenham cut him off, his tone reassuring.

"The government upholds the national interest above all. Do not concern yourself with the details, Roderick."

The voices moved on and Hetty ventured a quick glance

through the tree branches. Dear heavens, they were intent upon stringing up Sir Aubrey, even if they couldn't find what they needed to convict him. He might be a philanderer, and Hetty nothing more than one of his many conquests, but she couldn't see him hang for something he hadn't done.

Sliding into the walkway as a throng of revelers rounded the bend, she melted into the darkness, joining their straggling ranks as if she were one of them until she reached the hub of the park once more. The orchestra had struck up a lively piece by Mozart and as she cast her panicked look around, she was never more relieved to hear Araminta's voice.

"There you are, Hetty! Oh, and there's Cousin Seb, too, with Mary bringing up the rear. Goodness, that girl's sourer than ten-days-old milk. You'll find yourself a husband before she does, Hetty, if that's any consolation."

The only consolation Hetty felt at that moment—and it was considerable, nonetheless—was that she'd inadvertently timed her arrival at the moment the two disparate sets of cousins converged. Both groups seemed to assume she'd been with the other.

Araminta hooked elbows with her as they sauntered through the gardens, saying what a pity it was Hetty had chosen to abandon her and Stephen since Mr. Woking had accosted them not two minutes before, asking after her.

"Papa would be satisfied with such a match, for Mr. Woking's family has large landholdings in Hampshire and he's an only son. I doubt you could do better."

"But I don't like Mr. Woking," Hetty protested. "He has clammy hands and his breath really is most unpleasant." Though that was the least of her objections. Overhearing him and his uncle just now had left her in a difficult predicament.

Araminta affected a falsely disapproving look. "It sounds as if you're already far too familiar with Mr. Woking to possibly back out now." When Hetty tossed her head, Araminta said, more placatingly, "An ardent suitor is just what you need after Edgar's tragic death. Planning a wedding will take your mind off your grief and marrying Mr. Woking is just the ticket, I'd say."

Miserably, Hetty countered, "Then why don't you marry him if you think he's such a good catch and he's an only son and well connected?"

Araminta didn't hide her revulsion. "Not even if I were

desperate. No, I can do far better. Besides, as I've told you, I have my sights set on other quarry."

"Perhaps you think that if I marry Mr. Woking you'll have closer access to Lord Debenham. You can't use me like that, Araminta."

Araminta appeared to shift uncomfortably. "I've told you already, it's Sir Aubrey I'm interested in. And as for the slander Cousin Stephen harps upon, it doesn't worry me a jot. As long as he's received and he has money and a title, then he's handsome enough for me."

"What if Sir Aubrey does not wish to make you his wife?" Hetty was aware of her challenging tone. She did not like Araminta's sly smile.

"I have gained the impression on the several occasions we have been alone together that I am just the kind of wife he is after."

Her lips curved up even more at Hetty's gasp. Fortunately Araminta must have assumed it was shock at her boldness because her response sounded smug. "Dear Hetty, even an innocent debutante must take risks if she's to seize the advantage. I intend to marry Sir Aubrey before the year is out."

"You can't—"

Araminta raised her eyebrows and in the amused silence, Hetty struggled for a response. "I'd have imagined Lord Debenham held a greater attraction for you."

"Indeed, he is most intriguing with his brooding black looks and raven locks, his white skin and hawklike nose. If I'd call anyone dangerous, it would be Lord Debenham." A faint look of distaste marred her pretty features.

"Lord Debenham would have you believe that Sir Aubrey is the villain."

Ignoring this, Araminta replied sharply, "And I would have you try to foster a tendre in Lord Debenham's nephew. He looks sheep's eyes at you when you're not looking, you know."

"Sometimes, Araminta, you are so heartless it gives me a headache," Hetty whispered. Araminta frowned as if she did not understand her. "Heartless? My dear, I am doing everything I can to foster Mr. Woking's interest in you in order to ensure you don't end up a poor, discarded creature destined to play unpaid nursemaid to our parents as they grow old and feeble. For you do know that's what will happen if you become a confirmed spinster?"

"I'd rather that than become wife to Mr. Woking."

Araminta turned to wait for Stephen and the others. Gently chiding, she said, "You know you don't mean that, dearest. A September wedding, I'm predicting. You can borrow my goose-feather-trimmed bonnet that Aunt Sarah made me. I'm afraid it *makes* me look such a goose, which is why I've never worn it, but it'll please Aunt Sarah and I think that you'll feel more comfortable if you're overwhelmed by feathers and furbelows. Certainly that'll be the case if you're not exactly feeling overwhelmed with love—though I've heard that often comes with time.

"Ah, Stephen, Hetty was saying she has a headache so perhaps you can get the cousins to take her home so we can go on together to Lady Misshelene's ball-assembly. I distinctly heard Sir Aubrey mention he'd be there this evening."

Stephen slanted a concerned look at Hetty before regarding Araminta with suspicion, but Hetty had no heart for more entertainment.

Silently, she followed her lackluster cousins into the hackney carriage Stephen flagged down. Cousin Seb was showing distinct signs of queasiness by the time they passed their townhouse and wearily Hetty told them to have no concern for her as, with worried looks, they questioned the rightness of allowing her to continue the two blocks alone to her own lodgings.

But Hetty didn't care what became of her and waved aside as lip service their fears for her well-being over such a short distance, saying, "Judging by the bilious look on Cousin Seb's face, I think it's best to remove your brother earlier rather than later."

Cocooned in silence, Hetty reflected amidst the tumult of her feelings. Sir Aubrey was a scoundrel but she did not believe in her heart of hearts she'd fallen victim to a villain. In fact, the conversation she'd overheard outside the supper room suggested Sir Aubrey was facing a more immediate danger than he could know.

The more she dwelt upon it as the lonely clip clop of hooves rang upon the cobblestones, the greater became her concern. Sir Aubrey had no idea of the lengths to which his enemies would go to condemn him. Only Hetty knew. A great sense of destiny made her sit straight as she considered her options.

The hackney was nearly to her home but not three blocks away was Sir Aubrey's townhouse. He might not be there but he was in danger. She could warn him. She could distinguish herself by her boldness and daring.

Not by speaking to him and risking her reputation again, but she could ask for pen and paper to scribble him a note that would be delivered to him the moment he came in. She'd sign it so he knew that she was his benefactress.

For once Hetty could feel as if she were the star performer in her own adventure. A heroine. Yes, for once Hetty could play the heroine.

Chapter Five

A LARGE WAXING moon had Sir Aubrey waving away the lantern his footman rushed forward proffering. He didn't need any help from anyone.

Wearily, he climbed the stairs to his townhouse. He'd been a fool to have bespoken a supper box in Vauxhall Gardens, but it had been the second anniversary of Margaret's defection and Vauxhall was where he'd proposed marriage. For some maudlin reason he'd planned to drown his sorrows in claret. It had done nothing except make him dissatisfied and distinctly out of sorts.

Or maybe that odd little chit of Maggie Montgomery's had done that with her refusal to entertain him. She'd scampered across his path when he'd least expected it and completely disarmed him with her dimpled smile and plump white arms.

Recalling the image gave him the urge to enfold her in his arms and kiss her cheekiness into something far more primal.

It piqued him more than he cared to admit that she'd wriggled out of his amorous embrace. However there was something so endearing about her, he found himself dwelling on her often, which was strange since she was by no means as dashing as Jezebel, nor the beauty Margaret had been.

With her round, innocent face and her confident demeanor she was an enigma; part unworldly debutante, part brazen lightskirt. Perhaps she was a gentlewoman fallen on hard times. If so, she seemed oddly agreeable to his ministrations.

He cleared his mind of any further speculation. When it came to women, Sir Aubrey had a policy of probing no deeper than what they chose to present as part of their charade for his benefit. He didn't have time or energy to invest in any "fallen on hard times" or "ruined by the vicar" tales of woe. Whatever cards one was dealt, it was incumbent upon the individual to make the best of the situation. If that meant a woman was unexpectedly cast into his orbit, he would do the decent thing by her, show her what pleasure could be had, milk the situation for what was on offer and then move on.

Well, that had been the way the past twelve months or so had played out. He had discovered true love after he'd married Margaret. The string of associations since her death had done nothing to take the edge off his pain, though he prided himself on the fact no mistress had come after him with anger or vengeance in her heart. He always settled his dues.

He turned as he reached his front door, which was when he noticed a hackney loitering by the kitchen steps. Angrily he marched back down the steps and rapped loudly on the curtained window of the equipage. Expecting to surprise some gormless lackey employed by Debenham to monitor his movements, he was taken aback when a familiar cherubic face peered at him through the glass. "Good Lord!"

He wrenched open the door and she gazed out at him, her expression severe rather than inviting. "I was writing you a note, Sir Aubrey."

"Indeed." He thrust his arm into the dark interior. "Perhaps you'd care to come inside and explain why you felt a note was more desirable than your company." Despite his irony, he was exhilarated. She must have left Vauxhall and come promptly to his townhouse. Her lackluster response to him in the supper box had been part of the pretense.

"Come now and stop playing games. You'll catch your death of cold." He patted her gloved hand as he helped her out before paying the jarvey, and was even more amused by her apparent reluctance. As if she hadn't planned this from the start.

As he led her up the stairs to the front door, he was impressed at how well she played the young lady of fashion. Her dress, her mannerisms had been learned to a fine art. He dampened the flash of curiosity as to her origins, saying instead, "That's right. Dombey will take your things."

When she hesitated once inside the lobby, he chuckled. "It's too late to play the coy maiden now when you've already cast discretion to the winds. Up the stairs we go. That's right. Along that passage. I want to hear exactly what you're up to and what's in this note."

For a brief moment, she hesitated at the top of the stairs. As well she might, the little baggage, he thought almost fondly before suspicion gained the ascendant. Could she really be spying on him? Was it possible she'd been recruited by Lord Debenham?

As soon as they'd gained the sanctuary of his private quarters, she swung around to face him. "Let me make it plain, Sir Aubrey, I have no interest in further dealings between us other than to warn you that I believe you have enemies," she stated baldly. "That is why I am here."

The defiance of her tone and the way she squared her shoulders was so at odds with the soft and ladylike creature she presented in all other respects that he was quite taken by surprise. Dismissing his earlier suspicion she might be a spy, he almost hugged her to his chest.

Instead he tilted his head and replied with his usual heavy irony, "Indeed."

Trembling, she thrust something at him.

"Your dance card? Empty? Is this the device now employed by those who seek to emulate their betters? Hardly novel."

She glared. "I won't stay if you're going to make fun of me. I simply thought it might interest you to know I stumbled upon two gentlemen hiding in the bushes outside your supper room and overheard part of their conversation that concerned you, sir."

This shocked him though he tried to hide it. He hadn't wanted validation of his suspicions that his enemy was engaged in further eroding his standing. He thought a moment, wondering if it was perhaps he who was jumping to conclusions. Yet he was the injured party, after all. He had nothing to fear or hide. All anyone had to go on were rumors and he knew they could never be substantiated.

"Try another gambit, my dear—"

"Henrietta," she said. "Henrietta is my name."

He ignored her, gently pushing her so she fell backward onto the bed. "Like hiking up your skirts, dear Henrietta, so we can get to the business that really brought you here. It's the only way you're going to be paid, isn't it? And paid more than you would have for a quick fumble in the supper room. You're quite strategic, my dear. Admirable."

To his surprise, she struggled beneath him. Not the token struggle he was so used to but a concerted struggle, which made clear her objection to being taken in this way. He straightened and stepped back.

"What games are you playing now, poppet?" he asked. Suspiciously, he added, "If this is a ploy, I might remind you that Mrs Montgomery will be expecting more than her pound of flesh. I'll not be bled for more…unless you can offer me something very novel." He licked his lips.

"No!" she said quickly, shaking her head. "You took my virtue the other night, sir, and you introduced me to many wonderful feelings, but I will not be taken anytime like some common jezebel."

"Ah, Jezebel," he sighed, recalling his previous flighty and unlamented mistress before realizing that's not what she meant. "So what do you want?"

She looked uncertain, as if assessing the merits of continued intimacies. "Maybe you could talk to me first."

He let out a shout of laughter. "Of course, how careless and ungentlemanly I must seem. You were in too much of a hurry before but now that you have me when you want me, you'd like to pretend to be a lady. You want to show off the skills Maggie Montgomery taught you." He tugged on the bell rope that hung by the bed, adding, "You want to prove you can hold your knife and fork properly so that I might just consider making you Lady Henrietta. Ah, Briggs," he said to the sleepy lackey who answered his summons, "a bottle of champagne. Not my best but good enough for present company, eh?"

He quirked an eyebrow before grinning at the clearly fuming little miss before him. "What? You're offended I didn't order the finest my cellar has to offer? My dear, if I intended to make you my wife, I most certainly would have. Right now my intention is simply to take the edge off your objections so that you'll part your legs with all the obedience your calling requires of you."

She gasped, ducking with surprising agility beneath his restraining arm as she dashed for the door.

Realizing it was no act, he dragged her back, genuinely contrite and with the real fear that she might indeed leave when suddenly the success and enjoyment of his evening hinged upon her company.

"I apologize for my vulgarity." He truly did. This was not the way to speak to this young lady, and if she had once been respectable rather than spawn of the gutter—it was always impossible to tell with Mrs Montgomery's girls—she'd consider him perfectly vile. "Please stay." Gently, as if enticing a frightened animal, for she reminded him of a dear little fawn, he contoured her soft cheek with his forefinger. "If you are indeed a gentlewoman fallen on hard times—though let me be clear, I do not wish to know your history—my words show me up as the scoundrel I am."

"What does it matter if I were a gentlewoman fallen on hard times or a streetwalker who has never known better?" Her eyes flashed as she delivered her rebuke, though he noticed she closed her eyes at the physical contact rather than stepping back. "No real gentleman would speak in such a manner. I'm sorry, Sir Aubrey, but I really have no further desire to consort with you. I merely wish to inform you that you have enemies."

When he put both hands on her shoulders, her attempts to twist out of his grip were so genuine he did in fact believe she meant to follow through on complete resistance. It made him all the more determined to persuade her otherwise.

"I already know I have enemies, so that's nothing new." He did not believe she had any real information but he was happy to humor her. "Ah, here is our champagne. Pray, be seated, dear Henrietta, so you can furnish me with all the details your investigations have revealed."

He waved her to a chair, hiding his amusement at her narrow-eyed look as he indicated to the servant to pour two coupes of champagne.

"I find your excessive gallantry cloying. Your brutish vulgarity was almost preferable, sir."

"Is there no pleasing you?" he lamented with false despair as he took a seat facing her. He raised his glass. "To the satisfactory execution of whatever business propelled you here, my dear."

She took a sip, eyeing him suspiciously over the rim. "I don't know what that's supposed to mean." Coughing a little as the bubbles apparently tickled her nose, she added, "However I can assure you my intentions went no further than wishing to advise you of matters pertaining to your safety."

"Ah yes! Where were we in terms of this vile conspiracy against me that you fortuitously overheard? We are taking a very long time to get to the point."

"If you're not going to take me seriously, I might as well go now, sir."

"Oh, I take you very seriously, my dear." He allowed himself a wolfish smile as he raked her body with a slow, lascivious gaze. He was rather enjoying this game. "Indeed, if it can be proved that you have in fact saved me from whatever terrible threats hang over my head, I shall reward you handsomely."

"I don't want money."

He chuckled. "You're just here for the pleasure of my company. Of course, my dear."

She shrugged, putting down her empty glass with rather unsteady hands. "Would that surprise you?"

"Girls in your situation need to be strategic, I understand that, and I do not condemn you for it. We must barter what we have for what we want. You, no doubt, are looking for a rich and well-connected benefactor—and if you were clever enough, a title—meaning I would be just the ticket, wouldn't I?"

She tossed her head, though he saw her stifle a smile. "I could do better than you if I were patient enough."

"Oh, I'll not gainsay that, my dear." He stood up and moved 'round to stand at her shoulder, lowering his head to kiss her neck as he refilled her glass. "So you could do a lot better than me?" He handed her the fizzing liquid, then sighed. "Alas, you are right. I am not a man to whom a lady should ally herself if she has other options, for I shall retire the moment I am bored. If there is any possibility that your heart might get broken then I suggest you leave right now."

The dismay he read in her expression when she raised her head pleased him, for he fancied she was not playacting now. "Or rather, once our pleasant little session is over, for I confess I am rather looking forward to divesting you of your stockings and running my hands over your nicely turned limbs. You were well advised to delay proceedings so I might enjoy the pleasure of your diverting little mind. It's been quite a novelty. Now, come here and sit on my lap so that I might hear more about the danger I'm in."

She bit her lip and frowned. "I dare not, sir."

"You dare not?" he asked, resting his chin upon the nut-brown curls that cascaded from the top of her head. "That is what brought you here, is it not?" He dipped one hand into her bodice to toy with her small nipple. It hardened immediately. "What is it this time?"

Her gasp reverberated through him. "You will ruin me."

"Perhaps…if a child results." He kissed her earlobe before taking the little shell into his mouth. Her trembling increased. She was enjoying this, he could tell, and he didn't believe it was an act. "My dear, I am assiduous in employing means to prevent conception. I desire a child as little as you. You have my word that if such an accident were to happen I would hold myself responsible for the consequences—if it could be proved the bastard were mine."

Instead of rearing up indignantly at this, she said, softly, "I do not intend to give myself to anyone other than you, sir."

He felt rather pleased with himself. After an uncertain start he'd lulled her into an almost somnolent state. Once again he'd proved his prowess with the female species. He was looking forward to what the next hour would bring, more than he usually did.

* * *

Trying not to squirm too much on her little gilt chair, her hands clasped demurely in her lap, Hetty shivered as he stalked around to face her. In her experience of men, Araminta was the one to garner the kind of fascinated interest she was now enjoying.

Enjoying? If she was honest with herself, this was one of the highlights of her life. A handsome, desirable man was sizing her up and clearly did not find her wanting.

Common sense faded in and out between thrills of excitement. Three times at least during this exchange she'd been on the verge of bolting.

Now, once again, she was watching him advance like the predator he was and her mind was whirling. Would she allow him to have his wicked way with her all over again?

If she stayed she was courting ruin. Yet what difference did it make since she was, to all intents and purposes, ruined already?

Hetty was a romantic by heart, but nevertheless, a practical girl. It was perfectly possible she might never marry. Not with Araminta perpetually throwing her into the shade. What gentleman would marry Hetty when he'd forever be comparing the sisters and secretly acknowledging he got the plain and dumpy one? Well, there was Mr. Woking, but didn't that just highlight her point?

If she had to choose, she'd rather risk hell in the afterlife by taking her pleasures with this wicked, handsome rake than endure a dubiously rewarded life of virtue on earth, sharing a marriage bed with Mr. Woking. She didn't think she had the fortitude for that kind of life sentence. If he had bad breath, she knew with almost absolute certainty he must snore.

She gave a little hiccup and quickly put her hand to her mouth, feeling suddenly jaunty now that she'd made up her mind to court ruin and damnation when all was said and done. Indeed, it was a grand feeling, sitting here and watching Sir Aubrey smile at her with that deliciously wicked, self-satisfied smile. She'd never before made decisions that had such import on her own life.

Now that her vacillations had come down on the sinful side of the coin, she thought she might like to make him work for his pleasure.

"Well, sir, you have tutored me once in the ways of men and women and, as we both concede, ruined me in the process." She sent him an expectant look. "What else can you show me, to make my fall from grace worth the price?" Dear Lord, she could not believe herself capable of speaking so brazenly.

With feline grace, he reached for her hands, raising her to her feet.

Her heart began to thunder while a thousand butterflies seemed to flutter their wings against her most sensitive parts. She was so unused to the feelings holding her hostage she could barely breathe. Was this what she could expect every time she came into such close proximity with this man?

Gently he cupped her chin, bringing his lips down to meet her hers in the softest of kisses. Straining for more, she reached up on her tiptoes, tentatively running the tip of her tongue across the seam of his lips. She gasped when he lunged forward, enveloping her in his arms and plundering her mouth as his hands roamed over her curves. He wasn't gentle now and she didn't want him to be.

For the first time in her life, Hetty felt truly desired. Sir Aubrey was kissing her with relish, his expression one of rapture, as if her soft flesh and rounded breasts and buttocks were the stuff of his dreams. Would a husband like Mr. Woking make her feel like such a woman?

Foolish irrelevance, was her last conscious thought, swallowed by her soft moan as his mouth moved from hers to blaze a trail of kisses the length of her neck, continuing across her chest before coming into contact with her nipple. Pressure and passion had pushed it above the edge of her bodice, which, as he'd also deftly unfastened her gown at the back, now slithered down to her waist.

The gown was not needed, she decided, giving a little wriggle so that it pooled around her ankles. She stepped out of it, straining to keep her arms around Sir Aubrey's neck while she rained kisses upon the hollow of his throat.

In mutual ecstasy they swayed in one another's embrace, their sighs of rapture mingling with the hiss of the crackling, spitting fire that bathed the room in a comforting glow.

With a growl, Sir Aubrey whisked Hetty into his arms before tossing her onto the bed.

One moment she was gazing, no doubt like a startled fawn, into his lascivious, purposeful gaze, the next he was surging up from her ankles and taking her chemise up past her waist before appearing with a wicked grin between her legs.

"Sir Aubrey!" she squeaked, but her momentary embarrassment was swept away, leaving guilty pleasure in its wake as he parted the folds of her sex with one long sweep of his tongue. A rush of sensation roared through her, as intense as any she'd ever known, casting every particle of rational thought from her mind and leaving her boneless with lust. She existed only in the moment. The exquisite moment.

Heat prickled her skin and she closed her eyes, her mind spinning into a pleasurable, all-encompassing blackness as he gently massaged the growing nub at the center of her desire. It was both terrifying and exhilarating, for just as she felt herself on the verge of safety she was once again plunged into the void of dangerous bodily sensations. Sensations that made her feel increasingly out of control.

Her breath came in staccato gasps.

Startled by the sudden dip of the mattress beneath her, she opened her eyes to find herself staring into the satyr-like grin of Sir Aubrey, who'd divested himself of his breeches and who now rose above her. Hetty's fascinated gaze slid the length of him and her response must have reflected her true feelings when he chuckled, "So glad I'm not displeasing to you, madam." His eyes glittered as he caged her body with his, positioning himself at her entrance. "I'd not expected such unfettered eagerness from one so inexperienced."

"Oh, Sir Aubrey, you're magnificent," Hetty whispered, bracing herself with a mixture of fear and excitement. He hadn't hurt her before, which was rather astonishing considering how very large he was. Now she was primed as she never had been, her body throbbing to receive him; for he was a king amongst men in all his glorious nakedness, and all the more desirable for the palpable excitement she saw reflected in his expression.

Exhaling on a sigh of ecstasy as he plunged into her, Hetty was soon experiencing a plethora of very different emotions as he moved inside her.

He filled her completely—both her body and mind. The sensations caused by the friction of body parts were both alarming and intensely pleasurable.

"God, you feel so good!" he rasped, thrusting faster, his eyes glazed as if he were in the throes of ecstasy. She certainly was, and to see and feel the effect she had on this gorgeous man was gratifying in the extreme. The tension inside her was almost unbearable. Her breathlessness increased while the pounding between her legs was echoed by the pounding behind her breast.

It was exquisite torture. Sublime pleasure.

And she had no idea where it was going to end.

"Oh, Sir Aubrey!" she screamed as something inside her snapped and she spiraled out of control, unable to harness her bucking and thrusting. She was at the mercy of forces beyond her control as ecstasy took her hostage and blackness swirled through her brain.

"God, Henrietta!" he responded as his breathing became more rapid. So did his thrusting, until, on a cry of rapture, he seemed to explode, withdrawing just in time and collapsing, still holding her tightly.

Chapter Six

IT HAD ALWAYS been a source of tension that Araminta and Hetty had to share a lady's maid. That is, Araminta objected strongly to having to share. Hetty didn't mind.

This evening Jane was busy with the tongs and sugar water as she created a becoming coiffure for the younger of the sisters. She was a relatively new addition to the staff but her amiability, discretion and the fact she was as adept with a hairbrush as ensuring peace reigned in the Misses Partingtons' dressing room made her popular with most of the household.

With eyes closed, Hetty surrendered to Jane's ministrations and dreamed of Sir Aubrey with mixed feelings. Her current situation could not continue, she knew that. Exposure was a constant threat and she was a fool for courting discovery. Secretly she hugged the hope that she might supply the information Sir Aubrey needed to exonerate himself. Yet Hetty knew her ability to succeed in this arena was as unlikely as spinning straw into gold.

Araminta was pacing. "Are you nearly finished?" Her gusty sigh cut through the hitherto pleasurable silence. "I, too, have to present myself at Lady Kilmore's ball and I am the eldest."

Calmly, Jane countered, "I'd a' tended to you first, Miss Araminta, had you bin here. But since your sister were already at her dressing table it were only good sense to start on her toilette. Don't she look a right picture tonight? Reckon the London air agrees with you, Miss Henrietta."

Araminta grunted. "Well, if I'm to receive an offer I must be where I've said I'll be. Sir Aubrey is a busy man."

"Sir Aubrey, is it, Miss Araminta?" replied Jane, raising one eyebrow. She pursed her lips as she continued to sweep the bristles through Hetty's tresses.

Hetty found it easier not to betray her distress if she kept herself very still through the taunting of seemingly a thousand gargoyles who leered at her from the recesses of her brain. Could it really be true? She'd thought Araminta's aspersions regarding Sir Aubrey's supposed interest mere half truths. Yet if Araminta regarded Sir Aubrey as a suitor, what chance did Hetty have?

Naturally she'd never expected in a millennium that Sir Aubrey would make her an offer…

But she certainly had not expected Araminta might waltz away with such a prize.

It had happened with Cousin Edgar but she would not…no, she would not allow it to happen with Sir Aubrey.

When Jane threaded the silver fillet through her finished coiffure, Hetty rose, holding up the masquerade mask she was to wear that evening, fluttering her eyelashes as she tried for a tone of gaiety.

If indeed Sir Aubrey was pursuing Araminta, as her sister claimed, perhaps Hetty could gain greater insight into how matters really stood if she were in the guise of a king's consort from the previous century.

Straightening from a deep curtsy to affect a very uncharacteristically seductive sashay about the room, she said airily, "Tonight I shall enjoy watching you cast your lures, Araminta, but perhaps I will surprise you and snare the game from under your nose." Her gurgle of laughter was as much prompted by the ludicrousness of her managing such a thing as fear of Araminta's power.

Not surprisingly, Araminta, now occupying the dressing table stool as Jane worked on her hair, considered Hetty's words barely worthy of a response. Opening one eye she said lazily, "Whatever game you snare will only be on account of the fact that you're in masquerade."

Before Hetty could respond, Jane quickly intervened. "You both look *ravissement.*" The French adjective was incorrect and spoken with a strong East London twang, but Hetty appreciated Jane's peacemaking attempt. Impulsively she put her hands on Jane's shoulders and pulled her away from Araminta and into a twirl. Her spirits had bounced back. Tonight she would shine. Beside Araminta she'd never thought that possible, but tonight they were equals. Hetty's glossy brown ringlets would be looked upon as favorably as Araminta's raven tresses by some men, surely? She was another creature beneath the mask and the layers of makeup, hoops and petticoats.

Another creature who could reinvent herself in whatever form she desired.

"You've made me into a beauty, Jane, and I may just succeed where Araminta does not. What do you think?"

Clearly uncomfortable, Jane stepped out of her grasp and bent to pick up a dropped hairpin from the floor. "You'd best both beware of that Sir Aubrey," she said with a shrug. "Fancier fish to fry's all I can say."

Araminta, who'd leaned back in the chair with a look of utmost boredom as Hetty had purloined the diligent Jane, now opened her eyes. "Oh, do tell all, Jane!" She affected a hushed whisper. "How many wives has he locked away in his tower?"

"Can't rightly say, miss, only my…that is, a young man what I know told me 'bout him."

Araminta leaned forward and put her head close to the looking glass to inspect the fall of a ringlet from her temple. "Out with it, Jane, if you want to keep your job beyond Christmas."

Jane affected concentration in reordering the silver boxes and bottles lined up on the girls' dressing table. "Sorry, but I ain't one to gossip, miss," she whispered. "'Specially when it might cause harm."

"He's dangerous?" Araminta's eyes gleamed. Hetty wasn't surprised. She would have dropped the subject but her sister, jumping up from her chair and gripping Hetty's hand, demanded, "You're duty-bound to protect us, Jane. I promise your young man, whoever he is, will be safe."

It was only after prolonged interviewing that Jane conceded her admirer Jem was her source and that he happened to be valet to Lord Debenham.

Hetty's mouth dropped open. "Your young man is Lord Debenham's valet?"

Araminta sent her a sideways glance. "Are you sizing Lord Debenham up as your future husband, Hetty? He's very dashing, of course, but hardly the type who'd look your way, I'm afraid, dearest."

The magnitude of what she'd learned just now was too much for Hetty. "You are so unkind, Araminta," she declared, grasping her skirts as she made for the door. "I have no interest in Lord

Debenham."

"That's as well." Araminta returned her attention to her reflection. "I've heard he's a very dangerous gentleman. Just like Sir Aubrey. Best to steer clear of them both."

Hetty hesitated by the door. She didn't want to know what this Jem might have to say about Sir Aubrey, for she'd not believe it. Sir Aubrey was kind and gentle and passionate, all at the same time. He'd stroked and kissed her, made her feel fiercely desired then looked at her with a fondness that could not be feigned.

However, the possibility she'd felt earlier that she could in fact inveigle Sir Aubrey into some kind of legitimate union lay in shreds if Araminta was serious about making him a conquest.

She faced her sister fiercely, determined for once to have the last word. "Not if I'm to keep an eye on you, Araminta, and see you don't do something rash."

"I suppose you must find something entertaining with which to occupy yourself while you wait to be asked to stand up to dance."

Hetty nearly collided with the door as it was opened and the measured voice of her beloved mother resonated through the tense atmosphere.

"Why, Hetty, you look beautiful—though a little flushed."

Hetty flung herself into her arms, making the most of the brief comfort afforded by Lady Partington's embrace before she was set aside, her mother's affection now tempered with justified suspicion as to her elder daughter's behavior. "I hope you've not been suggesting to Hetty she won't be every bit as successful as you, Araminta." Lady Partington's gentle face was almost forbidding. "Hetty's kind and sweet nature count for a great deal when a gentleman weighs up all factors pertaining to the long future he must share with the woman he chooses for his wife."

Hetty wished she'd included something that alluded to Hetty's improved looks.

Her sister, now sitting on the edge of the bed, showed no sign of contrition. "I was only cautioning Hetty as it appears she's set her cap at Lord Debenham." Araminta's smile became cloying. "Without being unkind, Lord Debenham is quite simply out of her league, just as Sir Aubrey is—and besides, Sir Aubrey has made his interest in me clear so I'd hate to see Hetty wounded or, worse, regarded as a failure by the end of the season. If Hetty would only consider Mr. Woking—"

"Will you desist from this idea that I would consent in a thousand years to accept an offer from Mr. Woking?" Hetty cried, stamping her foot.

Araminta stopped with a look of exaggerated surprise before giving a couple desultory claps. "Bravo, Hetty. So you are capable of a spark of passion. Perhaps there's hope yet."

"Enough, girls!" Lady Partington stepped into the center of the room, holding one hand up for silence as if the girls were squabbling infants. "Pray tell me more, Araminta. *Are* you interested in this Sir Aubrey about whom I hear such unsavory rumors?"

Araminta displayed her pretty white teeth in a most ingenuous smile. "Mama, you've told me never to take rumor for the truth else half the ton's reputation would be in tatters. Why, if an otherwise eligible gentleman is considered unsuitable purely on account of a rumor, closer association must be the final arbiter." She cleared her throat delicately. "Certainly it must be in the absence of evidence to convict."

A small gasp escaped Jane and Lady Partington swung 'round. "And what do you know about all this, Jane?" she demanded.

Miserably, Jane toyed with the now-cold curling tongs. "I know the young man wot's valet to Lord Debenham, ma'am, and he said summat that made me afeared o' Sir Aubrey."

Hetty held her breath and hoped her expression didn't give her away as Jane went on. "Afeared of Lord Debenham too, only I weren't sure if I should say, seeing as how Miss Araminta is so taken."

"Well, that's dropping me in it!" Araminta hissed as she rose and took a turn about the room.

Hetty struggled to keep her expression bland as her mind whirled with possibilities. It could not be true. Well, the part about Sir Aubrey's villainy though she was thoroughly convinced about Lord Debenham's. Sir Aubrey had explained everything.

She heaved in a breath, forcing herself to hold on to the conviction that Sir Aubrey had been unfairly maligned. The alternative was too awful to contemplate. She could not risk losing herself to a villain, a reprobate.

The trouble was, she acknowledged with a little moan she tried to stifle, she already had.

Lady Partington arranged the folds of her dress around her as she lowered herself carefully onto the green and gold counterpane, stroking her large belly. "In the interests of my daughters' welfare, Jane, I must ask you to tell us everything you know." Concern furrowed her brow, replacing the fond maternal look she usually affected at such times. "You have my word there will be no repercussions for you or for your young man."

Jane nodded, opened her mouth to speak then, clearly reconsidering, said in a panicked voice, "Jem made me swear I'd tell no one. He said it could cost him his job. Nay, his life, even, if his secret got out."

Even Araminta showed surprise but Lady Partington was calm as she repeated, "Tell us now, please, Jane. You have all our assurances that no sources will be revealed."

Jane sniffed, shifted from one foot to the other, then finally said in a low voice, "Jem's bin valet to Debenham from the time 'e came back from the Far East, where he worked for the powerful East India Tradin' Company." Staring at her feet, she shook her head. "I don't know nothing of the East India Tradin' Company but I do know Lady Margaret's brother also worked for the East India Tradin' Company and that he were accused of something fearful, and that Lord Debenham and Lady Margaret were afeared what were goin' to happen to him." She rubbed her eyes with her knuckles.

"Where, exactly, does Sir Aubrey come into all this?" Lady Partington prompted gently.

"Well, m'lady, the story's this. When Sir Aubrey went away, his wife, Lady Margaret decided to visit her brother Master James, who were now living back in England. And it so happened that Lord Debenham also were visiting, cousins as they all were."

Hetty narrowed her eyes. His Lordship's visit had, according to Sir Aubrey's account, been anything but innocent. If this was the version put about by Jane's young man it didn't sound as if the truth were about to emerge.

"I do not think Sir Aubrey cared for Lord Debenham, who was too familiar with Lady Margaret," Hetty said.

Predictably, Araminta swung around. "How would you know such a thing?" she demanded but Lady Partington put up her hand for silence before signaling Jane to go on.

Even in the dim light the girl's sallow face showed her deep reluctance to speak of matters she'd been told were never to be discussed. She toyed with the corner of the cloth that covered the table on which the lamp sat.

"Jem says that on the final day of Lord Debenham's visit, His Lordship and Master James repaired to the library whereupon a great argument broke out," Jane continued. "In a fury, Mr. James went to seize his sword only Lord Debenham pulled out his own and wounded the young man mortal bad."

Hetty saw her mother's eyes widen as Araminta said in bored tones, "I fail to see what this has to do with Sir Aubrey."

Jane glared. "Well, Miss Margaret were naturally distraught at her brother's being so badly injured. Then Sir Aubrey arrived in a fury, claiming his wife were carrying on with Lord Debenham. Instead of going to Master James' aid, he turned on His Lordship and the two men began fighting and then Miss Margaret tried to stop them. Well, neither were hurt but when Lord Debenham went in search of Miss Margaret…"

Jane held up her hands in a gesture of defeat, prompting three voices to cry out in unison, "Well, what happened?"

"You know the story already." Jane nodded at them. "Lord Debenham found Miss Margaret in her dressing room while Sir Aubrey attended to her brother. Mr James were dead and…so was Lady Margaret. Quite dead, from the nightshade she'd taken and holding a note."

"You say there *was* a note? A letter that she'd written?" Hetty asked, her stomach lurching. "What did it say?"

Jane looked furtive. "Jem reckons it were saying Sir Aubrey had driven her to it through being a husband of such wicked and unkind ways. And other things about him being involved in that plot to knock off Lord Castlereagh besides."

"I doubt very much Jem can read," Araminta interrupted sharply. "So where is this letter, anyway, since it's the only means of verifying anything?"

Jane's eyes skittered indignantly to her interrogator. "Jem were with Lord Debenham after. His master were swearing somethin' terrible, pacing up and down the room and waving the letter in the air."

The chills that started at the tips of Hetty's toes rippled up through her body, forced out in a gasp as she implored Jane to go on.

So a letter did exist and it was last in Lord Debenham's keeping.

"Jem asked what were in the letter but the master paid him no mind at first. He were muttering that it brooked ill for himself if it were discovered but Jem were havin' a hard time catchin' what he were sayin'."

Hetty had to press her lips together to prevent herself from saying she had little wonder Lord Debenham didn't want the letter found.

Jane smoothed her cotton print skirts and continued her story. "'Is Lordship then told Jem the letter were all 'bout how Miss Margaret were so ill-used by her husband and were a testimonial to Sir Aubrey's evilness. Them were his very words." With a worried frown she fiddled with the curling on the dressing table then said with a squaring of her shoulders, "But that weren't what he said first time round. Anyway, the master took to the drink after that and Jem found him asleep with his head on the table and the letter just lying there."

Hetty knew she was weighing up whether to add more by the way she gnawed her lip. "So that's when Jem took the letter?" she surmised. "As his insurance?"

Jane sent her a frightened look. "What Jem did were a terrible thing and he's oft regretted it." There was a pleading note to her voice. "But Lord Debenham is a harsh master. He don't know if Jem has the letter or not but at least it keeps him from thrashing him or threatening him like before."

Lady Partington rose slowly. "So Sir Aubrey's reputation rests on what was…apparently…written in that letter."

Hetty could have hugged her. "Of course it does, which is why the letter must be made public." She turned to her mother. "Jane must urge Jem to hand over the letter, mustn't she, Mama?"

The response she received this time was disappointing. "Hetty dearest, these are the weighty matters that must be dealt with by those who are directly affected. Certainly I shall speak to Stephen about it. But as Sir Aubrey and Lord Debenham are gentlemen who hold no interest for you, I'd ask you to desist from taking this on as a mission of mercy." She patted Hetty's hand, saying more gently, "I know you love to see justice done and I'm so proud of the way you want to help those unable to fight their own battles, but Lord Debenham and Sir Aubrey are grown men and we're talking about serious matters right now. If you even mention that you know about this matter, it could be deeply damaging to both your reputations."

Hetty stared at the floor to hide her trembling lip. How could she ever explain to her mother what a vested interest she had?

Reality diminished the size of her role as potential savior. To Sir Aubrey, Hetty was nothing more than a woman of the night. She swallowed painfully, glad of the masquerade mask she raised to hide her devastation. If Sir Aubrey was after a wife, as Araminta suggested, it would be entirely plausible that he'd consider her beautiful older sister.

Jane's defense of "her Jem" filtered through the roaring in Hetty's ears. "'Sides, wouldn't you do all you could to protect yourself if you was in danger of losing not just your employment but your character?" the young maid demanded.

Hetty shuddered. She'd well and truly lost her character. But to a man who ill-used his wife? She couldn't countenance it. Indeed, she could barely countenance what she had reduced herself to, though to be honest, she didn't feel the guilt she ought to feel at having debased herself. Every time she thought about Sir Aubrey a frisson of desire surged through her. It left her breathless, shaking, exhilarated and...hopeful.

Yes, a small flame of hope still burned within her. Araminta was beautiful and beguiling. She'd entrap Sir Aubrey but Sir Aubrey was not a man who liked to be entrapped. He'd told Hetty so himself as he'd caressed her with murmurs of how refreshing it was to pleasure and indulge himself in such a sweet piece of innocence. He'd hinted that if he still thought the same in another month, he was going to set her up as his mistress.

She slanted a guilty look at her mother.

Araminta as his wife and Hetty as his mistress? No, that would never do.

But maybe, she thought, emboldened by Stephen's words of earlier, Sir Aubrey was not only a worthy suitor; maybe he'd consider a plain and accommodating debutante a more desirable lifelong partner than one full of spirit and fire such as Araminta.

Lady Partington rose and made for the door. "Girls, you both look beautiful, and I only wish I could be there to witness your success." She turned, her hand on the knob, and her smile gained warmth as she gazed upon her youngest. "Hetty, you look especially charming. You will break hearts tonight, I'd depend upon it."

***

At Lady Kilmore's ball later that evening, Hetty lurched from the veritable euphoria she'd felt at her mother's words to complete self-disgust. Through the slits of her mask, she drank in every detail of the well-dressed throng and for the first time didn't find herself wanting. The mere sight of Sir Aubrey's familiar tall, broad-shouldered form made her mouth feel dry and she longed to have it moistened by his wicked tongue.

He was dressed as a satyr with a curved cutlass angled over his emerald-green cummerbund and a patch over one eye, a contrast to Lord Debenham, who'd chosen a monk's cassock. Sir Aubrey's dark-brown curls were tousled and the ruffles of his white shirt were in disarray as if, Hetty thought fancifully, he'd been engaged in fierce rough- and-tumble with a dragon or a dangerous fellow satyr.

He did not hold a mask to his face as many others did. His eye patch sufficed, though of course it was the unusual contrasting streak of white hair against the dark that set him apart.

Hetty, on the other hand, was carefully inconspicuous in a damask full-skirted sacque gown adorned with bows and furbelows in the style favored the previous century. As a debutante she could not claim to style herself upon the infamous Madame du Barry, mistress to the former French king, but that's whom she imagined herself. The costume kept her identity well hidden. Her hair was powdered and a heart-shaped beauty spot was placed to the right of her mouth.

Araminta had remarked it was a shame Hetty hadn't lived in an era that allowed her to hide so much under layers of paint and flounces but Hetty had just laughed. That's what she intended to do when all was said and done. Have the last laugh. Araminta would not always get what she wanted at Hetty's expense. The difficulty would be in just how Hetty achieved it.

She ran through her plan once more. Tonight she would waylay Sir Aubrey and hint at having information he'd be glad of. She wanted to pique his interest by letting him know she was aware of the existence of the letter that Lord Debenham said revealed him a traitor and wife-beater. Of course Hetty would never dream of being alone with him again, much as she might desire it, but in masquerade it would be easier to find an opportunity of drawing him away. Just a whispered assignation in a corner with perhaps a stolen kiss and she'd be satisfied. Even if she'd now learned he *was* a wicked man. But that was the problem. How would she know—how would the world know—unless that letter were made public?

And that's where Hetty would come in. She would visit Jem and induce him to hand over the letter. If there were only some way she could slip unnoticed into Lord Debenham's townhouse while he was safely at Lady Kilmore's ball, she might have the matter well in hand by the morning.

Breathing heavily, she fanned herself as she relaxed against the support of the wall and closed her eyes. If it could be proved that Sir Aubrey's reputation had been wrongly tarnished, then Hetty would be his savior and who knew how he might choose to reward her?

When she opened eyes again it was to see the lithe figure of a water sprite dressed in the sheerest robe of aquamarine glide up to Sir Aubrey, tuck her hand into the crook of his arm and flutter her eyelashes at him.

Araminta.

The pain and jealousy, which Hetty had thus far successfully managed to hold at bay, took root and surged up her gullet. Indeed, it was several moments before she was in a position to rejoin the crowd and sidle up to Mrs. Monks, who was looking decidedly anxious.

"There you are, my girl," declared her chaperone, peering at her through her lorgnette. "Your mother has charged me with your good name and I'll not see you compromised by disappearing into any shadowed corners."

"You mean like Araminta and Sir Aubrey?" Hetty asked innocently. "I saw them not a moment ago and came to warn you, as he's a gentleman Mama is most concerned about. Naturally I couldn't go after them."

"Araminta? Why, she was just here..." Anxiously Mrs. Monks scanned the room until Hetty helpfully pointed out the pair in the process of slipping out of a side entrance.

Within a surprisingly short amount of time, Mrs. Monks had waylaid them with a frosty, "And pray tell me, Miss Araminta, what had you in mind?"

Chapter Seven

Hetty sidled into the shadows, excitement replacing the dismay she'd felt when she registered Sir Aubrey's warm gaze as he'd looked at Araminta. But then, Araminta was a brazen hussy and what man could resist the kind of enticements she'd dish out when she wanted something?

Well, she'd not get Sir Aubrey. Not for her husband. Hetty was determined upon it.

With Araminta now out of the way for a short while at least, Hetty just had to be patient until an appropriate time to approach him came along, meanwhile hoping he did not leave Lady Kilmore's ballroom and look for entertainment elsewhere.

Hetty's opportunity came unexpectedly. She'd been watching Sir Aubrey all evening with half an eye, ready to disappear if he ventured too close when she was amongst her peers. Tonight she was to all intents and purposes an imposter. A cypriot breaching civilized society. That's what Sir Aubrey must think when she made her approach. He would think her bold beyond belief. And she'd revel in being branded something so alien to her nature.

She picked up her skirts with one hand to glide across the room, patting her mask to ensure it was tied securely. It was strange to wear hoops and petticoats when she was used to the fine materials and narrow-skirted, high-waisted gowns she'd worn all her life.

As Sir Aubrey issued into the corridor, Hetty slid into his orbit. "Sir Aubrey, we meet again," she said breathlessly from the shadows. She removed her mask, having positioned herself a few yards along the corridor away from the open door that led into the ballroom. Laughing at his confusion, she added happily, "It is I, Henrietta."

"Good Lord!" he exclaimed, not without pleasure. "How on

earth did you slip past the gatekeeper?"

He strode forward then took her in his arms, chuckling as he stroked her cheek and contoured her curves. "You inhabit two worlds, my bold ingénue, and the mere proximity to what I have enjoyed but twice is sending me wild." He held her away from him as he regarded her with narrow-eyed amusement. "No doubt that was your intention. What is not so clear, however, is how you thought you might profit from this secret assignation. I cannot acknowledge you…indeed, I cannot be seen publicly with you."

He looked as if he were truly regretful.

Hetty nodded, sagging against him and sighing with pleasure as his exploring hands became bolder, slipping into her low-cut bodice to fondle her breasts. They were alone, she'd made sure of that, but the sound of the orchestra through the walls added to the excitement.

Heat flowed through her, pooling in her lower belly and making her moist at the contact. Sanity also seemed to have abandoned her and she'd have sunk to the floor in his embrace had he wished it.

"Dear Lord, but you rob me of all reason," he muttered into her hair as he molded her bottom. "Stop me here, for as it is I am unable to return to the ballroom." He gave a wry chuckle and put her away from him, shaking his head. "Look at the state I'm in."

Hetty put her hands to her mouth, embarrassed and amused to see the evidence of his arousal. "Oh, sir, did I really cause that?"

"Don't pretend such innocence with me when we already know each other so well, you little minx." His soft, full lips curved into a smile of fond exasperation before he pulled her into another hug. "Though that said, your innocence is my preserve. I paid handsomely for it."

Fear speared her. "You received a bill?"

"You know very well what a good businesswoman your Mrs Montgomery is. I will be presented with my bill at the end of the month and it will be paid promptly. Nothing less is expected. Oh yes, the tailor, the breecher, the mantua maker, they can all wait but Maggie Montgomery must receive her money on time."

Rapidly Hetty calculated that she had two weeks before discovery was inevitable. Such a calculation should not engage the numeracy skills of an innocent debutante wanting to make a good marriage, she conceded with a stab of fear. Nor should an innocent debutante have had reason to discover that there were two words to describe an "abbess" and that brothel-keeper was one.

Mistaking her look for something else, he was quick to reassure her. "My dear, I will pay it gladly, do not fret. I'm wild for you and if I could, I'd tup you right here and now." He cupped her pink cheeks. "Forgive my crudeness. It was intentional and purely so I could enjoy watching you effect your finely honed skills at playing the parson's daughter fallen on hard times." He jerked his head in the direction of the doorway. "Come, let us go now."

Hetty stepped back. "I can't, sir."

"Can't?" His supercilious eyebrows rose. "What prevents you? Surely that's the very reason you waylaid me? Indeed, it was my intention to send a message to Mrs Montgomery that I wanted you sent 'round to me this evening."

"Surely not, sir! I am glad I found you first, then, for I have spent the afternoon helping my near-blind papa prepare his Sunday sermon."

He chuckled, clearly enjoying their exchange as he wrapped his arms about her shoulders and led her a couple steps down the passage. "You are vastly diverting, my dear, the way you hint at hidden mysteries."

Hetty's grin faded. How much should she tell him? "Sir Aubrey, I have discovered something recently that I think you would very much like to know."

He chuckled again. "Is this a clever little ruse to gain extra blunt from me that your employer won't get her hands on? If so, I'm very amenable to any arrangement you might suggest." He tightened his grip upon her leaning down to kiss her deeply on the mouth. With a sigh Hetty wilted in his arms.

Her pulse was still racing when he set her back on her feet, murmuring, "Come to me tonight. I shall endeavor to be home by three. No, make that two a.m., for the anticipation is already killing me. I have other obligations in the meantime but you'll round off the evening nicely, my lovely Henrietta."

My lovely Henrietta. Hetty could only grin stupidly, her pleasure overwhelming despite his cavalier attitude. The knowledge that he thought her no more than a creature of the night was dispelled by the conviction that one day he'd know the truth—and not be disgusted by it.

Determined, she pushed her shoulders back. She had to find

a way to redeem herself. Make him understand she hadn't deliberately tricked him so that he would forgive her deception. Reward her for salvaging his reputation. For salvaging the reputation of the man who'd ruined hers...

"I shall try, sir," she said as she turned to go, the sudden fear that Mrs. Monks might march through the door overriding her previous high spirits. She must find Jane's young man Jem as soon as possible and induce him to give her the letter. Oh, how she'd love to be enfolded in Sir Aubrey's arms later tonight but while that wasn't possible, her mission might result in something infinitely more long-term.

Araminta didn't love Sir Aubrey but Hetty did. And this time Hetty was going to get her man.

Instead of issuing directly into the ballroom, Hetty turned toward the ladies' mending room, gasping as she brushed against a tall gentleman enveloped in a monk's cassock. He didn't stand aside but instead deliberately blocked the narrow corridor.

How long had Lord Debenham been there? What had he observed? Too fearful to raise her eyes, she murmured in quelling tones, "Excuse me, sir, I wish to pass."

"Ah, so the lady wishes to pass." With a bow, he stepped aside and Hetty glided toward the mending room, where she collapsed onto the banquette and, picking up the ivory fan beside her, tried vigorously to increase the circulation of air about her blazing face.

She was certain Lord Debenham was the only guest dressed as a monk. Had he recognized her? Dear Lord, whoever he was, he'd be following her every move now, for the irony of his tone indicated he'd observed her brief, passionate tryst with Sir Aubrey.

She tried to ease her fears. Even if she wasn't dressed in masquerade, anyone who'd ever seen her in company with her sister would certainly not have noticed a pale and unremarkable creature such as herself. Lord Debenham, well, he had an eye only for the dazzling. He'd never have known it was her. She was too far away and it had been too dark.

Breathing more calmly, she set her mind to finding a means to speak to Jem.

She knew Lord Debenham lived only two blocks from here. For that matter, Hetty lived just one block farther but distance wasn't the issue. How would she manage to slip away at any time of day? In the morning Araminta would want to engage Hetty in conversation that would emphasize her many successes of the previous the evening. Then there'd be luncheon. Hetty was a protected, nurtured single female and it would be impossible to leave their townhouse without an attendant, even for the shortest of walks.

It was as she was trailing through the ballroom beside Mrs. Monks that she saw Araminta bearing a beaming Mr. Woking in her wake, and a wild plan borne of desperation took shape.

Affecting an attitude of the greatest languor, Hetty preempted the conversation with, "My dear Araminta, Mr. Woking, you must excuse me but I have the most terrible megrim. I can't stay here another minute in this close and stifling atmosphere. I'm afraid I shall have to ask Mrs. Monks to take us home."

Horror replaced Araminta's smugness. "How can you be so selfish, Hetty? I'm having the most marvelous time and my dance card is completely full."

Hetty pursed her lips. "I suppose you could stay if Cousin Stephen didn't mind accompanying me home and then Mrs. Monks could remain here to chaperone you."

"I daresay that would be all right," Araminta said sulkily, ignoring the crestfallen young man at her side until she fixed him with a dazzling look. "Mr. Woking, won't you fetch me another champagne?" She tapped him playfully on his shoulder epaulettes with her fan. "You were so busy admiring my sister you didn't notice my glass was empty, did you?"

Hetty made certain she was gone before Mr. Woking could return with refreshments. She and a none-too-displeased Stephen hired a hackney and Hetty was treated to a long monologue on Stephen's concern about her mother's health, which surprised but also pleased her. Not least because it was nice when anyone spoke with such thoughtfulness of her greatly unappreciated and darling mother, but also because her cousin would be less likely to notice her agitation if he was so concerned with his benefactor's wife.

They were nearing the entrance to St. James Street where Stephen's club was located when she leaned across and put her hand on Stephen's knee. "You've got the blue devils for some reason, Cousin Stephen, and I think it's my cousinly duty to set you off here so you can drown your sorrows with company more exciting than mine."

"But what about—"

She cut him off with a laugh he'd surely peg as being brittle and unnatural had he not been caught up in his own concerns. "You can almost see where I live from where you are. No, why not get out here, Cousin Stephen, for in less than a minute I'll be home."

To her annoyance, he refused to let her go on alone and soon they were drawing up in front of her townhouse.

He assisted her out, saw her to the front door, then turned, declaring her idea a capital one but adding he'd rather enjoy the fresh air and walk to his club.

A glance over her shoulder as Hetty was about to issue through the front door showed Stephen, head bent, deep in thought as he trod the footpath. The bright moon also revealed the jarvey upon the box, taking his time as he retied his muffler.

Hetty dashed back down the steps and rapped lightly on the carriage door to garner the jarvey's attention before whispering, "Stay there another minute. I've just remembered something."

The housemaid who'd answered the door was waiting at the top of the steps and Hetty quickly returned to explain that Mr. Cranbourne had left an important document in the carriage and that she would return it to him, then prevail upon Mr. Cranbourne to return to the ball with her.

"He is, after all, less than one hundred yards away," she assured the servant, pointing. Indeed, he was in sight, not yet having rounded the bend.

Minutes later, Hetty was descending the steps to the basement of Lord Debenham's townhouse, patting her mask to ensure her identity was properly concealed.

The sleepy-eyed scullery maid who'd obviously been roused from her makeshift bed near the fireplace regarded her with slack-jawed amazement as she clearly tried to peg Hetty as a streetwalker or eccentric lady of quality, while Hetty repeated in clipped tones, "Mr. Jem, your master's valet. That's whom I've come to see. Surely he's not abed yet since he has his master to attend and Lord Debenham won't be home for some hours, I believe."

A handsome young man with delicate features and hair the color of corn answered the summons. He regarded Hetty quizzically from the kitchen doorway before ushering her into the servants' hall. When Hetty told Jem she had a matter of the utmost importance to discuss, he waved away his fellow servants but mention of the letter wiped the smile from his face.

"You realize any magistrate would take a dim view of what you've done," she told him as he folded his lean, athletic frame into a chair opposite her. "You stole Lady Margaret's death note. That's punishable by transportation at the very least."

Jem wiped at the sheen that coated his high forehead. "Only one person knows about the letter," he muttered. "I can't believe—"

"It really doesn't matter who told me since you won't be facing any consequences except rather good ones, I'd imagine, if you cooperate." Hetty smiled as she clasped her hands upon the refectory table. "Of course, if you pretend ignorance I shall have to have you cross-examined and you know the courts are very skilled at detecting if someone is lying. They might decide you are anyway and convict you just on Lord Debenham's testimony."

"He'd not dare." Anger flashed from his pale-blue eyes. Suddenly he leaned back, smiling as if he understood everything. "Me master's set you up to this, hasn't he? Reckon he put the word on you when 'is own threats had no sway wi' me." He shook his head decisively. "I ain't no fool. Far as I'm concerned, there ain't no letter so I don't know what you're talking about."

Hetty sighed before coming to a decision. "All right, I'll tell you the truth. I have a personal interest in Sir Aubrey and when I heard of a letter that might exonerate him I set upon discovering its whereabouts."

Frowning, Jem raked his eyes over her. A faint sneer curled his lip. "So you're Sir Aubrey's fancy piece? Did 'e set you up to this?"

"He did not and I am not his 'fancy piece', as you term it." Hetty strove for dignity. "I have a great tenderness for Sir Aubrey. I understand the painful association between his wife and your master. Worse, I know that it is solely due to Lord Debenham's lies regarding the contents of this letter that Sir Aubrey's reputation has been so sorely damaged."

A slow grin split Jem's handsome face and his eyes glittered. Almost collaboratively he leaned across the table. "You reckon you 'ave a lot to gain by finding this evidence, don't you?" He quirked an eyebrow. "Reckon also you'd be willing to pay for it too. It won't come cheap, yer know." Hetty's anticipation was only slightly dented when he added, "No doubt you earn a pretty penny doing your line o' business but this'll cost more than even the best o' your sort can pay."

She knew she could afford his fee but she waited for him to negotiate.

"I'll let you peruse it. I ain't givin' that letter to someone I don't know from Adam." He looked so determined Hetty didn't know how to start to argue but was relieved at the concession when he added, "If it contains the information you're after, your fine gennelmun protector Sir Aubrey can come to me direct and pay me what it's really worth."

A date was set for two days later, since that was Jem's half day and the letter was hidden at a location some distance from Lord Debenham's townhouse.

Then the young man rose, calling for the weary scullery maid, whom he instructed to "see the lady out".

Hetty followed the girl through the dim interior, the street lighter shouting the midnight hour as she opened the door onto the cobblestones. It was still early by Araminta's standards, which meant Hetty would be home and fast asleep by the time her sister returned.

"What an unexpected surprise."

Emerging onto the pavement, Hetty jerked her head up to see Lord Debenham issuing from his carriage and about to mount his portico steps.

He took a step toward her, pushing back his cowl and offering her a leer. "If it isn't Sir Aubrey's... 'special indulgence'. Come to indulge *me* now? I'm honored."

Hetty lifted her skirts to flee but before she could dart out of his path, he gripped her arm and jerked her to him. His cassock was rough against her cheek and she could smell the brandy on his breath.

"Where are you going in such a hurry when I've only just arrived, little one?"

His mouth was inches from hers and her insides cleaved as his malevolent intent became clear, his fingers biting painfully into her arm.

"I trust you did not satisfy yourself with the dregs in my basement when you failed to find me. No? Good, for I think if you can pass muster with those in Lady Kilmore's drawing room you'd hardly be satisfied with my fine valet, handsome though he is."

"Please let me go, sir." Hetty hated the sound of her own whimper. In a moment he'd hustle her inside and no amount of screaming would save her, for he was master of his own home.

"Surely you understand I'm curious as to why Sir Aubrey's little ladybird should interest herself in my business."

Cursing herself for her stupid recklessness, Hetty tried to pull away but her distress only added to his enjoyment.

"Let us not conduct business upon the pavement, madam. A glass of Madeira might make you more willing to please me."

Hetty made one last effort to depart with dignity, ceasing her resistance to say with a gracious smile, "Sadly, my business here, which was merely to stop in upon an old friend, is done and I'd hate to keep you from your bed——"

"Indeed, madam, my bed is where I intend to discuss what brings you here. Do not play the shocked gentlewoman with me. I saw how cleverly you infiltrated the ranks of the nobility and then witnessed you and Sir Aubrey in the back corridors of Lady Kilmore's. As it's rare to see Sir Aubrey so excited by a woman, you can be assured I'll not let you go lightly. Now come."

"No, sir, please!" Gasping, Hetty pulled herself free for but a second before Lord Debenham dragged her back against him.

"Who are you to say no to me?" he snarled, pinioning her against the railing. "Scream all you like but who do you think will come to the aid of a creature like you? If you offer Sir Aubrey your body for a price, I am entitled to the same—and for the same price. Business is business, is it not? And then you'll oblige me by telling me what brought you here."

Hetty could barely breathe through her fear. How had she sunk so low? Yet whatever happened and however ghastly it was, she had only herself to blame.

Wildly she fought, her scream truncated by his lips, hard, wet and determined, fastening on her mouth, his one hand gripping her chin painfully, the other snaking 'round behind her to grasp her buttocks.

His proximity was so invasive and his determination so intense her knees buckled. It only gave him greater access to the body he obviously felt was free for the taking.

Twisting her head away, she tried to scream again but he was too quick and canny for her, clamping his hand over her mouth before replacing it with his hateful lips once more.

She managed to suck in air, just enough to keep from choking. She tried to claw at him but he deftly forestalled her, gripping her wrist and pinning her arm to her side.

As she sank to her knees in a heap by the cast-iron railing, he scooped her into his arms, no doubt about to whisk her to somewhere he could continue his fiendish act less publicly.

"What are you doing with my woman?" The icy tone cut the air like a lash.

Dazed and breathless, Hetty clung to the railing, unable to speak as Lord Debenham set her back upon her feet, though her knees immediately buckled and she sank to the pavement.

"Your woman?" With heavy irony he continued, "Then why did she come to me? Poor Sir Aubrey. It's not the first time either, is it?"

Hetty, recovering quickly, was about to refute this when she realized he was not referring to her. Sir Aubrey hauled her up but his eyes met hers with anger, not sympathy.

"I thought we had an agreement," he muttered.

"You can't think that I would sink so low as to—"

"Debenham offered you more? Revenge, my dear Henrietta, but of course that would mean nothing to you, would it? Money is money, isn't it, whether it's mine or his, and if he's paying double…"

He was clearly too angry to continue, while Hetty, unable to reply, tried not to choke on her stifled sobs as he hustled her into his waiting carriage.

Lord Debenham's mocking laughter followed them as the door closed, his parting words: "Damsels in distress have always been your weakness, Sir Aubrey. Pity they all seem to prefer me," making him white with fury.

Lurching forward as the carriage rolled away, Hetty burst out, "I didn't solicit Lord Debenham's advances."

In the dim lamplight, Sir Aubrey's expression was thunderous. "Indeed, madam? You lost your way, did you? Just as you lost your way when you visited my bedchamber the first time. You made a fool of me, turning me into a purring pussycat in order to 'tutor' you. You weren't a virgin, were you, yet you would have me believe that—"

"Please, sir, you're far too angry to hear me out but I would *never—"*

"Stoop so low for money? That's not what concerns me here." He cut her off, glaring at her. "We had an agreement. It was based on honor. I thought even women like you understood the notion of honor."

Hetty drew in a sobbing breath. "I didn't visit his home to...to do what you think," she cried. "I went there because I heard about—" She cut the words short as her brain whirled over the ramifications of revealing the whereabouts of the letter. If Sir Aubrey learned Jem had it, he would demand to see it immediately and no doubt the young man would deny possession, knowing the likely consequences. Hetty was a soft touch. If the price was right, he had nothing to lose by allowing her only to view it. But he'd not hand it over when confronted by a belligerent Sir Aubrey.

Besides, it was essential for Hetty to know exactly what Lady Margaret had revealed about her husband. Hetty's future hinged upon it.

"Heard about what?"

Hetty shook her head, trying to think clearly. Wiping away her tears, she demanded, "Couldn't you see I was fighting him off? Your townhouse is only a block away. I was on my way to see you. I had no idea this was where ...Lord Debenham lives and I had no idea what an evil man he is or that he'd recognized me having observed us in the corridor at the ball this evening. He wanted...revenge." She sniffed and her voice trembled even more as she added, "And clearly I was the means of exacting it."

She was relieved to see that he seemed to believe her for his expression grew very dark and hands quite tender as he gripped her shoulders.

Hetty put her head on one side and decided not to be too forgiving too soon. "Yes! He told me he'd seen the two of us together at Lady Kilmore's. So, Sir Aubrey, since I was almost dragged off by this horrible creature against my will and all on account of the fact he saw you kissing me, perhaps you'd care to elaborate on the enmity between the two of you. Is there more to it than what you've told me?"

Sir Aubrey's tone was contrite when he finally spoke. "Hetty, I apologize for my anger just now." He dropped his hands and took both of hers which he began to chafe gently while he explained. "My late wife was this man's cousin." He looked bleak. "I'm afraid

76

she was also his lover. She was not of sound mind when she killed herself but Lord Debenham blames me."

Finally the shock seemed to sink in. What a terrible experience it had been to suffer the unwanted attentions of the odious Lord Debenham. But thank the Lord that Sir Aubrey still thought the best of her and that he was concerned, now, not angry. Hurling herself into his arms, Hetty sobbed, "I didn't mean to get myself into trouble like that and I'm so, so glad you saved me—just in time!"

* * *

How pleasant it was to sink into a soft feather mattress and feel his arms about her while he navigated his way past her hoops, petticoats and chemise. A single lighted candle suffused the room in a soft glow and his voice was infinitely calming.

His breath tickled her ear as he pulled her against his side. "My poor Henrietta has had a great shock." Touching his lips to hers, he stroked her cheek. His eyes, which could blaze with such anger, were warm with affection. "I don't deny some think a woman who makes her living like you do should be prepared for any manner of approaches and have lost the right to discern, but no woman ought to suffer unwanted advances."

He stopped Hetty's gasp of distress with another kiss, deeper and more demanding this time as his hands roamed her body, caressing her curves, her rounded buttocks as he rucked up her skirts. She raised herself to give him access, reveling in the flood of warmth such contact brought. Tenderly, he gazed down at her, smiling his satisfaction at her sighs and gentle moans.

"I thought you might like that," he whispered as he gently rubbed the raised bud of her sex, his desire to please her evident as he experimented with different approaches to stirring her blood. "What about this? No? Then what about this?"

His tongue circled her areola, flicking over her nipple and causing her to arch her back in pleasure. She cupped his face against her breasts, kissing his soft, dark hair and thinking this must be the closest to heaven she'd ever get, for she surely had lost her ticket there if being good and virtuous was a requirement.

She didn't care. She was never going to find happiness through marriage. She should know her desperate optimism was based on the flimsiest of hopes.

He was a considerate lover. She knew that, even though she had no one with whom to compare. After he'd fully aroused her, he undressed her carefully, admiring each piece of skin, each limb he uncovered, and when he had her completely naked he gazed at her appreciatively.

"No one has ever looked at me like that," she murmured, touching his cheek as he knelt to position himself at her entrance. He was huge and her insides churned with excitement and the need for him. She swallowed, watching the concentration on his face as he caged her with his lean, muscled body. "Plain Hetty is what they call me." Though Wicked Hetty was a more apt moniker. She didn't care. Her temperature had soared and her heart was pounding, sweat prickled her skin and she wriggled, parting her legs and pushing forward so that his shaft was suddenly buried within her.

"Magnificent Hetty." He exhaled on a groan before driving into her in a series of quick, eager thrusts that had them climaxing together within moments.

He laughed when his breathing had subsided and he pulled her against him. "I usually last longer than that. What spell have you cast upon me, my marvelous work in progress? For I think you might have remained Plain Hetty had you not fallen into my hands in the nick of time."

The kiss he planted on her lips was tender but within minutes he was ravishing her once more with double the enthusiasm of their previous proceedings.

Later, in the quiet aftermath of their lovemaking, Hetty idly stroked his lean torso while he, misinterpreting her silence, said, "Have no fears. I shall instruct Mrs Montgomery to release you from your contract so that I might continue to enjoy you exclusively. I find you utterly charming and I want to keep you safe, my little Henrietta." He looked thoughtful as he toyed with her right nipple, making her squirm. "At the first opportunity I shall call upon your good mistress and discharge my obligations to her. Then I shall install you in some charming bower so I can enjoy you whenever I wish."

The contemplation of such a scenario fortunately blinded him to her shocked response and by the time he returned his gaze to hers, she'd mastered herself. "Before you say a word, my enchanting Henrietta, let me repeat my assertion that I have no need to know why you chose this path, though I do not imagine it was something you embarked upon lightly—"

Oh Lord. Yes, she'd chosen her path. By accident, it was true, but she'd been mistress of her destiny from the start. The astonishing sense of power she found in making her own decisions had propelled her onward. Whoever would have imagined Miss Henrietta Partington was capable of such boldness?

"I don't ever want to be with another man," she whispered urgently and the idea that this would all come to a terrible finale brought tears to her eyes.

He toyed with her hair as they lay curled in each other's arms. "Truth be told, I'm too fond of you to see that happen...and I don't want to share you."

Of course he was not asking her to marry him, he wanted her to be his mistress. But a man chose a mistress because he desired her.

His wife he would choose for dynastic reasons.

"Mrs Montgomery is out of town until the end of next week," Hetty managed weakly, hoping her lame response would give her the time she needed to extricate herself from the consequences of her lies.

"Then as soon as she returns, I'll arrange terms by which you'll be entirely my responsibility. In fact, your wish is my desire. Tomorrow you shall accompany me in search of a townhouse where you shall have everything just as you like it."

He was eager to please her, which was delightful, however matters were proceeding rather too fast.

"What is it?" he asked, concerned by her lack of enthusiasm.

"I...I've heard men can discard their mistresses at any time. What...what security will I have?"

There was uncertainty in his laugh. "I'm assuming innocence, not avarice, motivated your question."

Fortunately he seemed entirely mollified when she declared, "I told you I only ever want you!"

"Just as I want only you. I do not offer my affections lightly, dear heart, but you have worked your way under my guard."

Pleasure washed through her before it was diluted by concern. Without censoring her thoughts, she said nervously, "I've heard there's a Miss Araminta Partington who has caught your eye. Perhaps you were thinking of marrying her."

Sir Aubrey laughed, shaking his head. "She'd eat me for breakfast. No, dearest Hetty, you are all I want and need."

"One day you will want an heir," she said softly.

He put his finger to her lips. "Now is not the time to talk of such things. Suffice to say that Miss Partington, while exceedingly beautiful, fails to amuse me as you do with your artless ways and your diverting conversation. Dear heart, I look forward to dining with you each night and hearing of your latest shopping exploits as much as I look forward to bedding you, for you would imbue both with wit and enthusiasm. Miss Partington, on the other hand, thinks only of her own amusement. I could not endure a wife like that."

Hetty had never been so happy. But she had mixed feelings when he added, "Sadly, darling Henrietta, you embody all the virtues I seek in a wife." There was genuine regret in his expression before he feathered a line of kisses along her jawbone. "However you must understand that I can never marry you."

Chapter Eight

Fortune favored Hetty as she crept into the kitchen unobserved several hours later, for the sleepy boot boy had left the kitchen door open. The cook was not yet about and Hetty met none of the servants as she slipped into her bedchamber.

Araminta was asleep, so Hetty was able to sink wearily beneath the bedcovers, relieved her clandestine activities had once again gone unnoticed.

Her last waking thought was that she wished she didn't have to wait another two whole days before Jem could meet her. For her entire future hinged upon what was revealed in the letter he'd promised to show her.

It seemed only five minutes had passed before Araminta was pulling her hair and saying in outraged tones, "No sleeping cap? How low your standards have fallen, Hetty."

Hetty braced herself for Araminta's inevitable grilling before her sister sat heavily on the side of the bed, saying waspishly, "You and Cousin Stephen certainly had lots to talk about, despite your megrim. I heard the two of you in the study. I hope you don't imagine he'll consider making you an offer, for he's already declared he will not marry his cousin."

Still groggy, Hetty murmured, "Like you, Araminta, I'm sure I won't receive an offer in my first season."

Araminta ignored this, though the flare in her eyes indicated the jibe had not gone unheeded. She rose, saying airily, "Mama and I are going for a walk a little later and Papa is down from The Grange. He arrived when we were at Lady Kilmore's and says he wants to see you. He was vastly put out you'd not made the effort to greet him at breakfast."

"I didn't know he was here."

"Well, he's taken it as a grave insult. Of course he knew not to expect me, since I was up so late, but you came home early and talked all night with Cousin Stephen." Hetty raised her eyebrows, wondering who Cousin Stephen had been talking to, but she wasn't about to tell her sister it wasn't her. "I came home because the close air at Lady Kilmore's made me ill." Hetty glared at Araminta. "And maybe I still am. You didn't trouble yourself to inquire, Araminta, did you?"

"Well…" Araminta had moved to sit at the dressing table by this time. Even after such a late night and in dishabille, which was a refashioned old gown of their mother's and which of course she'd not be seen wearing in public, Araminta looked vibrant and exquisite. "Jane would have told us if there was anything to worry about. But you're as hale and hearty as a dependable old donkey, Hetty. We've always said it."

The description had been given Hetty by a fond uncle many years ago and it still had the power to wound. He'd described Araminta as resembling a glossy, raven-coated, highly strung magnificent stallion and Hetty as the faithful donkey whose dependability made up for its unremarkable dung-colored hide. Oh, he'd meant it kindly, for his point was that he preferred dependability over uncertainty any day. Needless to say, Araminta had taken it as a compliment and was happy to bring it up in front of Hetty whenever the occasion arose.

It was only the memory of Sir Aubrey's disparaging remarks about Araminta the previous night and the fact he wanted exclusive rights to Hetty—even if it wasn't in the form of a legal union—that enabled Hetty to crawl out of bed in a cloud of joy, despite her sister's unkind reference.

A joy short-lived, for as she put her shawl about her, Araminta, who was toying with her hair, announced, "Sir Aubrey has invited me to promenade with him this afternoon." She sent Hetty a sly look from beneath her lashes as she twisted her neck, clearly interested in Hetty's response, which was obviously transparent.

Affecting a show of sympathy, Araminta reached over and patted her arm. "Poor Hetty, I know you've admired Sir Aubrey from afar and indeed I can see why but he's never asked you to dance or paid his addresses in the ballroom, has he?" She placed several pairs of kidskin gloves on the dressing table and held out her hands to admire her long, elegant fingers. "I can't imagine how dreadful it must be to be so plain that you're ignored by the one gentleman you evince a desire to know. Or should I say the two, for perhaps you think Lord Debenham might be your consolation prize since you seem to know so much about him too."

With a sigh, she rose from the dressing table, adding with even greater self-absorption than usual, "I've been thinking…" She cupped her face with her hands as if her thoughts had plunged her onto the horns of a dilemma. "Do you think my sprigged muslin will do for my outing with Sir Aubrey or would you recommend my blue sarcenet? I've heard you say it sets off my coloring rather finely."

"I only said that when you'd not leave me alone without saying something flattering," Hetty muttered.

But Araminta wasn't listening.

"The sprigged muslin, I think," she said as she wandered to the door. "It's refreshingly modest at the same time as being highly modish." She turned. "And I think it would be a nice idea if you popped your head in to see if Mama needs anything. You seem to have rather neglected her lately."

"Is she all right?" Hetty asked anxiously.

Araminta shrugged. "She was fine when she went to bed last night so I can't imagine anything's changed. Now I must find Jane and ask her to see if my walking boots have been cleaned. I shall be highly annoyed if they haven't."

Hetty heaved a sigh of relief when Araminta left her to her own musings and ablutions.

The excitement that had consumed her earlier became a weight of doubt and misery. Sir Aubrey had pledged to go walking with Araminta this afternoon? What sort of betrayal was that? Was he not supposed to be choosing a house today where he could visit her?

Anxiety curdled in her belly. By all that was great and good, how was she going to get around that one? Very well, he'd said he preferred Hetty and perhaps he did. But Araminta was the sister he was able to meet respectably in public and Hetty was the secret.

The lying, deceiving sister.

Unable to settle, she paced the room, chewing her fingernails as she thought how little time she had to extricate herself gracefully from the mess she'd created.

Tomorrow when she met Jem, she told herself, everything

would magically resolve itself.

* * *

To her surprise, her father greeted her with a great show of fondness when she stepped into the drawing room. Fondness and a surprising degree of admiration.

"My dear Hetty, but you are blooming," he told her as he put his hands on her shoulders to study her more closely. "You're turning into a beauty before my eyes. Isn't she, Sybil?"

Araminta, seated in a chair by the window, flicked a page of The Lady's Magazine she was idly perusing and said, "A couple of people have remarked upon it but she still hasn't the figure to fit into any of my clothes. Mama, what do you think of this walking dress?" She tapped a fashion plate in front of her. "I could have it made up in blue. Blue sets off the sheen of my hair. Sir Aubrey remarked upon it the other night. You know he is escorting me on a walk through Hyde Park tomorrow afternoon."

"I thought Mama said you were not to associate with Sir Aubrey," Hetty said balefully.

"What's this?" Lord Partington, now ensconced in a leather armchair, looked up from the newspaper he'd just opened. "Sir Aubrey? The fellow whose wife took her own life after he was mixed up in the Castlereagh affair a year or so ago?" His complexion turned a noticeable shade darker.

"Nothing was proved." Hetty spoke the words so sharply all heads turned on her.

"Stephen will accompany you," Lady Partington said in decided tones. "I shall send a note 'round to him this morning. If he knows it's important, he'll put aside whatever he's doing."

Her husband harrumphed as he turned the page he was reading. "I'm sure all it will require is a note from you, my love, and he'll come running."

Hetty noted his tone with surprise but Araminta had moved on to other topics. Namely the entertainments to which she'd been invited. "Of course I'll see that the invitations are extended to Hetty."

Araminta smiled warmly at her, though some of the gloss was taken off by her next words. "Papa is right, you are looking a good deal better these days and it's my duty to ensure that you are noticed, also, Hetty."

Ensure that she was noticed? It was a painful truth that Hetty had been overlooked for most of her life, having a sister like Araminta, but Hetty wasn't sure that now was quite the time she wanted to be noticed.

Surprisingly, Lord Partington evinced a desire to take a walk with his wife and two daughters just after luncheon. Hetty didn't think such a thing had ever happened before but as the sky was a clear azure blue and the breeze fresh and fragrant, she supposed her father was motivated by the weather.

In fact it was so they'd not be overheard by the servants.

"Several things have happened since you girls came to London, which has necessitated my going away for a while." He cleared his throat and stared straight ahead as they made their progress along the busy pavement.

Hetty glanced at him. His complexion was unusually ruddy— a deepened reddish hue not caused by the outdoors. And while his wife had fixed her gaze upon him, he seemed unable to meet her eye.

Hetty was surprised when her mother said, more sharply now, "It's high time you told the girls, Humphrey."

After further throat-clearing and prevaricating, Lord Partington got to the point. "The truth is, there have been several financial difficulties at home—"

Lady Partington cut in. "Both financial and domestic. Let's not beat about the bush, Humphrey. The girls need to know so they can be prepared."

Their father's shoulders slumped and his chin nearly touched his chest. Doggedly, he continued walking, forcing the others to keep pace.

Araminta was the first to speak, or rather gasp, "It won't affect my dress allowance or my portion, will it, Papa?"

More loud throat clearing was little comfort and it was their mother who explained in crisp tones, "Your father has made a rather large and unwise financial decision. His man of business is not entirely despondent, however, until—"

Hetty put a comforting hand on her mother's while Araminta wailed, "We're ruined! Is that what you're saying, Papa? We're ruined and we'll have to go out and work as governesses unless we marry quickly." There was both genuine distress and craftiness in her expression as she cut into her parents' responses. "Before the scandal breaks, we must find husbands, isn't that what you're saying?"

"Well, now, Araminta, while there may be some truth in—" her father began, but Araminta had already come up with a solution.

Looking decidedly more cheerful, she said, "I shall do my part, Papa. In fact I solemnly vow that I'll have made a grand match before two weeks is up so you need not concern yourself over me." She pinched Hetty's arm. "Now you, also, must make sacrifices, Hetty, but instead of being a governess, which would be such a terrible reflection on the family—and since you've made it plain you'll have nothing to do with Mr. Woking, who would offer for you if you only smiled at him—I know that old Lady Fotheringay is looking for a companion." She looked expectantly at Hetty. "I know her niece so I shall make inquiries—"

Their father cut in, his voice raised in both anger and exasperation. "Neither of you will make the kind of sacrifices that will see you wed in haste to unsuitable husbands or forced to work for your livings." In an undertone, he added, "Sadly, I have seen that fate visited on undeserving young women. I will not have my...nobly-born daughters soiling their hands. Bear in mind that you enjoy a status that accords you privileges denied your less fortunate sisters."

"Indeed you do," Lady Partington said, also under her breath, and Hetty glanced at the two of them. She'd assumed, naturally, that her father spoke figuratively, and he may well have, but then remembered having overheard a couple of gossiping dowagers in a quiet corner of a ballroom referring to "Lord Partington's secret brood". Until Hetty had become more acquainted with the ways of the world, the whispered conversation had made no sense.

Now she narrowed her eyes as she wondered if indeed her father was making a more literal reference to this "other" family. This second secret family he was unable to protect and fund as he did his legitimate one?

Without warning she was visited by a memory of the young woman who'd visited The Grange several months earlier on the pretext of finding favor for a school in the village. She'd borne an uncanny resemblance to Araminta. Of course, Hetty could not question her father at the time but as he'd farewelled this young woman, Hetty had heard him say under his breath that she'd been wrong to come to the house.

Araminta sniffed. "Whatever is required of me, Papa, I shall do it gladly." She broke off, a dazzling smile dispersing her air of tragedy. "Goodness! Here's Sir Aubrey! What a coincidence." Then, under her breath, "Mama, Papa, this is a wonderful opportunity for you to amend your opinion." She raised her hand in greeting, calling out, just as Hetty registered what was happening and before she knew what to do to save herself, "Good afternoon, Sir Aubrey."

Araminta inclined her head demurely while Hetty, beside her, hung back in horror, praying that her sister's glorious smile and the floral festooning of her hat would be sufficient to render her invisible.

Heat prickled the back of her neck and swept in ripples up from her feet as she clenched her fists and kept her head down. *Please dearest Lord,* she silently prayed, *don't let him notice me.* This had to be the stuff of her greatest nightmares. In a crowded ballroom she could have slipped away but here, in the street and hemmed in by her family, her real identity was never more apparent.

As usual, Araminta stole the attention with her busy chatter. Hetty bent down on the pretext of adjusting her boot. When she rose it was to find herself staring fully into Sir Aubrey's surprised then horrified face.

"Sir Aubrey," she acknowledged, making a small curtsy, her shame weighing her down so heavily she was surprised she was able to rise.

Araminta, still chattering, did not seem to notice that her handsome potential suitor had eyes only for Hetty. She gripped his forearm briefly, saying flirtatiously, "You look well, Sir Aubrey. Perhaps you've been riding. I certainly enjoy a good ride. But how lovely for you to meet papa who is down from The Grange for a few days attending to business. His arrival last night was quite a surprise."

"Quite a surprise." Sir Aubrey's echo was lackluster as he simply stared at Hetty.

A blackbird called from the leafy arbor above them.

Lady Partington filled the awkward silence. "I believe you hail from Hampshire, Sir Aubrey. My cousin is on familiar terms with members of your family. Mr. and Mrs. Dorian Waddington."

"You refer to my aunt and uncle. Quiet people who don't seek out London revels as I do, my lady." There was a twist to his mouth. Almost a warning, Hetty might have imagined, that hinted at the danger he posed. That he enjoyed living up to his reputation.

Lady Partington raised her eyebrows at his less than friendly tone. "So you enjoy London then?"

"There's so much to see and do and experience, I don't know where to start," gushed Araminta. "Though of course, an unmarried young lady is very restricted."

"Indeed."

The word was accompanied by a short but very well-aimed look at Hetty who, quailing, dropped her gaze to her half-kid boots. She wished the pavement would open up and she'd disappear into a puff of smoke, never to suffer the consequences of this terrible, terrible conversation.

Clapping her hands, Araminta raised her flushed and happy face. "I hear you've acquired a new phaeton, Sir Aubrey. Instead of going walking, perhaps you're looking for an opportunity to put it through its paces? This afternoon, even?"

Her bold inquiry received a lukewarm response, though Sir Aubrey clearly felt good manners made it incumbent to offer an invitation.

"Then Hetty will accompany her sister." Lord Partington looked dark. "I will not have tongues wagging."

Araminta simpered. "Wagging tongues? Oh, Papa, you are droll."

Hetty noticed that Sir Aubrey seemed to find this as droll as her father. The thunderous scowl on his face was not a good sign. Indeed it was not. No, her hopes and

"In fact, Stephen shall accompany both you girls, and you may take it in turns to drive around the park." Lord Partington's frown deepened.

There was apparently no argument to be had about this and Araminta, despite her initial cajoling, was left with a petulant lower lip until she decided it was no doubt wise to end the walk with her usual charm.

"Sir Aubrey is fantastically rich," she gushed once he had made a polite bow and departed with the trite and clearly forced words that he was looking forward to their meeting in several hours. "And he's in line for a title if his cousin doesn't sire an heir— which it's highly likely he won't as he's ancient. Fifty, I believe."

Her mother cut her off, saying coolly, "So you would risk your happiness for the sake of elevation?" Her pursed mouth trembled. "So that you can dress in ermine and silk rather than commoner stuff? So that you can drive around in a crested carriage?"

Araminta looked rather taken aback—as, indeed, her father did—before muttering, "I would only risk my happiness if I failed to hold him, Mother, and I'm cleverer than that." Her smile did not reach her eyes and there was a strange note to her voice when she added, "Do not underestimate what I know of the world."

"Neither your mother nor I would do such a thing." There was still no sign of Lord Partington's good humor. He put a heavy hand upon Hetty's shoulder, adding, "Though we sometimes wish you were a little less worldly and more like your sister. Hetty will make a sensible match, for she will be ruled by her head, not her heart, and be the happier for it. Think on that, Araminta. I say, Hetty, you're suddenly very pale."

"I...I don't know what's come over me." In fact, Hetty wondered if she'd survive the walk home. "I must lie down."

"You look worse than Banquo's ghost, Hetty!" Araminta exclaimed. "I don't think you'll be well enough for a ride in Sir Aubrey's phaeton after all. Well, we should turn back now anyway since I must decide upon my carriage dress."

Her self-absorbed chatter was the only bright note on their return journey. "I'd planned to wear this one for my promenade with Sir Aubrey but as he's already seen it, I shall impress him in my coquelicot. This one is rather demure. What do you think, Hetty? Do you think Sir Aubrey is the kind of gentleman to prefer boldness or shall I in fact wear my simple sprigged muslin?"

"Oh, I wish you would, darling." Her mother sighed. "You know, girls, Humphrey, I'm afraid I really am not feeling quite the thing either. Hetty, perhaps you and I should both lie down when we return."

"No doubt, my dear," said their father, "you'll be feeling well enough to entertain Cousin Stephen when he arrives to take Araminta." Hetty noticed his odd tone. Lord Partington sent his wife a piercing look. "By all means, send a note 'round to him. I've no doubt he will oblige. Meanwhile, I shall call on an acquaintance at the Inns of Court."

"How nice, Humphrey," said Lady Partington gaily. "And yes, I'm sure I will be quite well enough to entertain Cousin Stephen. Hetty, we shall have a lovely coze while Jane sees that Araminta is as dazzling for Sir Aubrey as she needs to be." She paused. "His family *are* respectable people but I am nevertheless concerned about these rumors, Hetty, unsubstantiated as they are. I heard Lord Nugent say that Sir Aubrey's political aspirations have gained no traction on account of this smear upon his name. Araminta, are you certain you wish to further your acquaintance with the gentleman when there are so many others dangling after you?"

"Oh, I do." Araminta leveled a determined gaze upon Hetty, who thought she was going to be ill on the spot.

What could she do? Her worst nightmare was being compounded by her second worst nightmare. Sir Aubrey had discovered her real identity and now Araminta was about to focus the full force of her determined charm upon him. Hetty hadn't a hope. If, as was remotely possible, he offered for her out of honor for having defiled her, he'd despise her forevermore. But, as was more likely, he would be as most men and wilt before Araminta's deadly charm, the moment Hetty reminded him he was not to blame for her deception.

Later, as she worked at her embroidery trying not to cry, she went over her options. She wished she could pour out everything to her mother, who sat beside her stitching a tiny garment for her new baby. Lady Partington, however, seemed not in the mood for conversation, though she rallied surprisingly when Cousin Stephen joined them.

"You're early." She smiled warmly. "Araminta will not be down for a while yet. You know how she is when she wants to impress, and indeed, she wishes to impress Sir Aubrey. Won't you have some tea?"

Cousin Stephen waved away her attempts at playing hostess, rather like a mother hen, Hetty thought. "The teapot is heavy and leaning over like that isn't good in your condition, Lady Sybil." When he saw Hetty's look he added somewhat sheepishly, "I'm forever in your mother's debt. I would so hate to see her come to harm on my account."

"Pouring tea?"

Clearing his voice, Stephen changed the subject. "I'm also reluctant to countenance this carriage ride. Araminta should not embroil herself with Sir Aubrey given his reputation. Who knows what she'll get up to when she has him alone in his phaeton." He grinned at Hetty. "You, I am not worried about. Hetty, are you sure you're not well enough to accompany your sister after all?"

Hetty sighed. "I'll go."

It was in this mood of resigned despair that she changed her own dress, barely conscious of what Jane laid out for her, her mind roiling with confusion.

Nothing was as it seemed. Her father apparently teetered on the verge of ruin. She was burdened by a terrible secret. And her mother and cousin seemed suddenly far too fond of one another.

Jane put her head around the door, her expression sympathetic. "Miss Hetty, you are poorly, aren't you? Let me fetch you something."

Hetty shook her head as she sank onto the dressing table stool. "Just brush my hair, please, Jane. You have such a soothing touch."

"That's nicer than what your sister can come up with, miss, when she wants cosseting."

No doubt Araminta had offended Jane once again.

Jane picked up the brush. "I wish Miss Araminta would stay clear of that fearful Sir Aubrey."

Hetty took the plunge. "He's a gentleman, a good man, Jane, and I intend to furnish proof that your Jem's master, Lord Debenham, has made it his mission to blacken Sir Aubrey's reputation by falsifying his account of what was in Lady Margaret's death letter." She turned when Jane's brush strokes faltered, saying eagerly, "Jem promised to show me the letter when we arranged to meet."

"Oh miss!" Jane dropped the brush and clapped her hand to her mouth as she stepped backwards, looking like Hetty had just struck her. "You never said anything to him, did ye? Oh, miss, now he'll know it were me what told his secret. He won't ever forgive me." When she began to cry, Hetty didn't know what to do. She felt guilty for Jane's distress yet fired with the zeal that justice would serve them all in the end.

"It's all right, Jane," she reassured her, reaching forward to give her wrists a comforting squeeze. "I told him he'd be handsomely rewarded. And he shall be."

"He's guilty of a crime and now he'll pay for it." Jane was sobbing now, having pulled free and collapsed against the window embrasure. "And I'll pay for it too. I swore I'd say nuffink to no one but then when I heard you and Miss Araminta talking I couldn't stay silent." She let out her breath in a whoosh of reproach. "Oh, Miss Hetty, I wish you hadn't told him."

Hetty couldn't meet her eye. She prayed Jane and Jem would not be added to her growing list of regrets.

"Please lay out my new muslin, Jane," she said bracingly. "I shan't save it for tomorrow musical soiree as I'd planned."

Too much hinged on this afternoon's expedition and she needed to look her most innocent and charming.

There was so much she had to put to rights. Whether she possessed the power of allure and words to work a miracle, only time would tell.

* * *

Sir Aubrey was not in a pretty mood as he flicked the ribbons over his pair of handsome bays. This should have been a proud moment. Right now, by this morning's calculations, he should have been a man who'd set himself up nicely. Just the right horseflesh and equipage to cut a dash and stir the blood out in the fresh air before returning home to sweet, undemanding domesticity.

Undemanding domesticity. It's what he'd envisaged would be the foundation of his first marriage, fool that he was for not considering the ramifications of marrying a woman rumor had it was mad for her cousin.

Arrogance? Innocence.

He rather thought that could excuse it. He'd never experienced the pangs of love or even a particularly strong desire for a woman before the necessity arose to take a wife. A marriage was a contract of expediency. This had been so well and truly drummed into him he did not think to question it.

When he'd met Margaret, he'd been struck first by her pretty face and sweet nature. He'd looked forward to a long and fruitful partnership. Men took mistresses when the unions with their wives proved unhappy but he'd been determined to be a good husband. A pity he'd not considered her feelings might have been engaged by another. Margaret's father had agreed with alacrity to the contract and Sir Aubrey didn't think to wonder if she had objections, callow youth that he'd been.

When Margaret lay cold in the ground, ruling out the possibility of reconciliation that had long sustained him, Sir Aubrey realized her death had created a vacuum that would be filled with pain and loneliness unless he found a long-term mistress, for he was not a man who would consider satisfying his sexual needs with a string of meaningless encounters.

Jezebel was as far removed from Margaret as was possible.

Jezebel. What a beauty. He was an object of envy for snaring such a rare gem. But with her beauty came a nature that was feisty, demanding and ungrateful.

His life became even more complicated as the rumors surrounding his wife's death grew. There were whispers that Margaret had taken her life because he'd driven her to it. He knew Debenham fed the flames, that he hinted Sir Aubrey had had some involvement in Spencean activities, including the plot to assassinate Lord Castlereagh.

He'd assumed such talk would be dismissed in the absence of proof. He'd been wrong. Debenham had influential friends and mud stuck.

Frustrated in his attempts to gain public office, Sir Aubrey had diverted his energies toward activities that were venal and self-serving rather than the lucrative and mentally rewarding positions within government he'd left his life as a country squire to pursue.

Meeting the two Miss Partingtons this morning was yet another betrayal. More proof that human beings were treacherous creatures and few of them—especially shy, innocent debutantes—what they seemed.

He heaved in a breath as he approached the trio that was to be his afternoon's entertainment. The gentleman among them, Stephen Cranbourne, eyed him with the suspicion of someone who knows courtesy requires that he be civil to an adversary whose soul is black with sin. His look suggested he was waiting for an opportunity to prove it. The dark-haired and most striking of the two young ladies simpered up at him with transparent design. Sir Aubrey had a fortune and would likely as not inherit a title. Miss Partington was brash and bold enough not to concern herself with his apparently dangerous reputation.

Her pale and unassuming sister was the enigma. Beside Miss Araminta Partington, no one looked twice at Miss Henrietta in a ballroom crowded with beauties.

And yet she was the one who had captured his heart. Captivated him.

He tried not to look at her while he considered the question. *Had* she really captivated him? When he'd entered into the liaison, she'd been little more than a business transaction. He'd bought her affections and her exclusivity and he'd thought confidently that his physical, and to an extent emotional, involvement were not matters that need concern him unduly until he was moved to change his circumstances.

Something in his chest cavity seemed to give a little. To crumple. He clamped his jaw down hard to stop his weakness from showing. The truth was, he had been captivated by her.

More. He had fallen in love.

As he pulled on the reigns and drew up beside the waiting party, his pain and confusion grew. To what purpose had his Henrietta—or rather *Miss* Henrietta—deceived him? It was unfathomable. Had she thought to force him to the altar by declaring publicly he'd taken her virtue?

Was she in fact a minion of Lord Debenham's?

To look at the downcast set of her features, her slumped shoulders and patent discomfort and embarrassment, he could countenance neither of these things.

"Hetty and I shall wait here in the shade." There was no friendliness in Stephen Cranbourne's tone as Sir Aubrey helped Miss Partington up beside him. Sir Aubrey was equally cool as he prepared to defend himself against his new companion's wiles. She was terrifying with her not-so-secret agenda.

He could barely make eye contact with the other one.

The other one. She'd have accompanied her elder sister everywhere, to every dance and every ball while he, blind to her less showy attributes, must have looked through her a dozen times.

"You're very serious, Sir Aubrey," Miss Partington teased him as she settled herself beside him, just a little too close for comfort. "I trust you are not concerned as to how to control your handsome bays?"

"I am not." He might have added more lightly that he was a

dab hand with the ribbons and so set the course for more entertaining chatter, but he could not bring himself to lighten the mood. Leave that to her.

Unfazed, she said after some minutes, "I shall want a pair of matched roans. My favorite horse was a roan. I'm very partial to them. I am an excellent horsewoman, Sir Aubrey. I believe you are fond of the hunt. So am I."

"Is that so, Miss Partington? Sadly, I am a busy man and do not spend as much time enjoying such pursuits as I might like."

"Then that must change, Sir Aubrey. Indeed, I have noticed you looking decidedly preoccupied these past few days and can only think that your work is too absorbing. It will profit you nothing if you are so joyless you cannot find a healthy sense of balance in your life."

"Balance, Miss Partington?" He glanced at her as they picked up speed and rounded a corner. "I think when we want something sufficiently we can find any means to justify it. Right now, I cannot justify pleasure when my reputation is besmirched by the rumors flying about me, and which I can't believe someone as percipient as you have not heard. I'm surprised you would be seen with me."

He'd hoped to repel her. At least put her off her stroke with the reference to his dubious reputation. To his dismay, her look of cloying self-satisfaction suddenly turned impassioned.

"Do not think I am swayed by evil, unfounded rumors! You have enemies, clearly, Sir Aubrey, and if they can be brought down, you will be vindicated." She reached out a hand, which he did not take, pretending a need to control the horses. She gripped his wrist. "You are a brave, *good* man and soon all the world will know it!"

He grunted. "Your sentiment is unfounded, Miss Partington. I am not a good man and you'd do well to remember it. See the concerned look in your cousin's eye as we return? It is fully justified. I am a rogue and you'd do well to steer well clear of me. Now, good day. I apologize for my ill mood. Your sister would be wise not to enter into discourse with me if she's of a timid nature."

* * *

Pique replaced Hetty's trepidation after Araminta jumped down from the phaeton, saying brightly, "Hetty, dearest, perhaps you should politely decline the offer of a ride with Sir Aubrey, since he says he fears he's not to be trusted to be civil and is bound to upset you in his present thunderous mood."

Just wait until they we're out of sight, thought Hetty with a surge of feeling as Sir Aubrey helped her, with obvious reluctance, up beside him.

For the moment she would not playact for the benefit of her sister and cousin, who might have been curious as to why the pair departed, stone-faced and staring straight ahead, but she would say her piece when the chance presented itself.

By the time they were well into the park, she'd prepared a spirited defense, but Sir Aubrey caught her off guard.

"You don't look like the sort up for that kind of lark, Miss Henrietta." He slanted a cold look across at her. "When am I to be revealed for the vile seducer you have unwittingly made of me?"

Of course Sir Aubrey thought she'd set out to trick him into marriage.

Hetty took a deep breath to still her rapidly beating heart then said in a low, dignified voice, "You bear no blame whatsoever. It was entirely my doing. But believe me, sir, I did not enter into the charade with anything other than a desire to save my skin, for I was certain you were going to slit my throat that first night."

His obvious horror made her gut twist. It was easier, she found, to look at the passing equipages on the sandy circuit rather than at him but at last she had to answer his inevitable question.

Sighing, she turned to face him. "When Cousin Stephen caught me watching you at Lady Kilmore's ball, he warned me you were a dangerous man. He insinuated you had a secret that was so terrible you'd do anything to keep it."

"A secret? Pray go on."

Hetty didn't want to go into the details right now. They both knew what they were. She shrugged. His eyes bored into hers with flinty purpose and how she wished she had the words and means to turn them limpid with love. She'd grown used to fond caresses and loving looks. His cold anger was more terrible than anything she could have imagined. Haltingly, she went on. "After I was in the lady's mending room I took a wrong turn, which led me to your chamber. The door was open and I was curious, for I'd recognized your cane—"

"My cane? How did you know it was my cane?"

"Well, it's very distinctive and I'd admired you from afar for a long time so I knew it well." She bit her lip. "But until that night I'd not known you'd kill to protect your secrets—"

"Kill? Good god, you know very well I spoke jestingly. Nor have I any secrets!"

"Well, you can't blame me for believing at the time what was said of you. When I lost my way and saw the door to your chamber open, curiosity got the better of me. Then you returned—"

He grunted then said in tones laced with irony, "And I was so fearsome you told me you were a lady of the night."

Hetty raised her eyebrows as she looked at him. "In case you've forgotten, sir, your shirtsleeves were covered in blood. You told me you'd just killed your assailant. I'd been given the impression you were hiding a secret so terrible you would kill to protect it so I simply agreed with your assumption I was there on legitimate purposes." She cleared her throat. "Well, as legitimate a purpose like that can be if I were supposedly a lady of the night."

His scowl deepened, his horror even more patent. "Dear God, you really thought I might murder you. But I *told* you I'd just fought off a dog that was about to tear my throat out—"

"You did not!" Hetty drew back her shoulders. "You *insinuated* it wasn't as bad as I thought, but that was later."

"I was in a foul mood, I do not excuse that. But for you, a respectable young lady, a virgin, to be so terrified you'd succumb to my less-than-loving advances…"

He could not go on and Hetty, who was becoming increasingly distressed by his response, said quickly, "But they *were* loving. And you were transformed from the frightening, angry gentleman into one who showed kindness and consideration. No man had ever looked twice at me but the fact that the very one whom I'd admired ever since I came to London *did* in fact notice me made me behave in a way that was quite…out of character."

"Yes, indeed it seems to have," he muttered.

Hetty clasped her hands and raised her face to his. "So while it's true that I'd started off being terrified of you and your reputation, I could have objected and told you the truth. I realised I could have but I didn't. So it was all my fault."

"Dear god, but you succumbed because you were terrified of me!" he repeated. His face was dark with an emotion she couldn't quite interpret but there were very large quantities of both anger and dismay.

"You succumbed to me because you feared me! You just admitted it! It was the only reason you had anything to do with me."

Hetty twisted her gloved hands. In a small voice she said, "I succumbed because I wanted to. And I came back to you...for more, didn't I?"

"Ha!" He shook his head and his lip curled as he snapped the reins. "I'd ruined you already. What choice did you have? You were led by your innocence and your fear."

"No, sir, by my heart—"

"Then all the more reason to wish for nothing more to do with me. I'll only destroy your illusions. I'll break your heart and you'll soon come to hate me."

"I won't have the chance if I'm never to see you again."

He'd been staring loftily ahead. Now his head whipped 'round. "That all depends on..." His tone gentled. "I have ruined you, Miss Henrietta, and as a gentleman I am required to save your honor." For what seemed a very long time he looked broodingly ahead of him, over the tops of the horses' heads. Then he signed ponderously before turning to face her. "Miss Henrietta, I offer you two choices." He slowed the horses to a gentle trot. "Marriage," he paused ominously, "offered with deep reluctance. Or, if you get out of this free of scandal, then the choice I favor, a clean parting of the ways."

Devastated, Hetty stared back at him. "So you would marry me if I desired it?"

He huffed out a breath. "I just said I would. I am a gentleman. I will not see you ruined. I would, however, wish you a better future than that. One without me."

"You would marry me but you would withhold your heart? What foolishness."

He nodded again. "I would leave you in the country the moment I could and live up to my reputation as a heartless villain. You would have every material possession I had the means to grant you but," he tapped his heart, "I would have nothing to offer you here, Hetty."

Hetty bit her trembling lip. Tears threatened. Not because he'd just offered her what she thought she'd desired more than anything else in the world: marriage. But because of his inability to see the emptiness of his offer. "You were going to set me up in a pretty house so you could visit me whenever you wished. Yesterday you wanted me. Desired me."

"Yesterday I was acting like a man who knows he can discard his mistress the moment he tires of her," he responded coldly. "A wife is not such an easily dispensed-with commodity and I would not build up your hopes in the early days when infatuation is based on falsehood, only to see you suffer more acutely for your blind faith later."

"That's not how it would be," she whispered. "You know it's not."

They were nearing the home straight. Stephen and Araminta could be seen in the distance.

Sir Aubrey fixed her with an intense look. "So what's it to be? Marriage?"

The greatest, loneliest feeling she'd ever experienced seeped through her. Slowly, Hetty shook her head. "I cannot hold you to something that is such anathema to you, even if it would give me the greatest joy to prove you wrong."

She drew in a quavering breath. "From the start, I knew Araminta was the sister you would choose. Goodbye, Sir Aubrey. You have my blessing, and my wish for your great happiness."

* * *

"Well, Sir Aubrey was in a less than pretty mood this afternoon," Araminta remarked once Hetty was set down and their erstwhile host departed with the requisite courtesies, namely a terse farewell for the girls and a frosty nod directed at Stephen.

Hetty clung to Stephen's arm, Araminta on his other as he navigated them through the well-dressed crowd. Stephen seemed not to notice Hetty's distraction. "No doubt having the very time of it trying to decide which of you to choose since you both for some extraordinary reason favor his advances," he said.

Hetty gave a little hiccup and both pairs of eyes turned to her. "Good Lord, Hetty, don't tell me you're cast down about it?" asked Stephen while Araminta let out a little trill.

"I can't believe, Hetty, you think he'd seriously consider you! Why, you're the absolute opposite of everything he finds attractive."

"And what do you know about that?" Stephen asked in dampening tones when he saw Hetty's distress. "Do you not think

Sir Aubrey would be as charmed by your kind and self-effacing sister as he would a showy piece? I'm sure he must be tired of young women throwing themselves at him."

He sent Araminta a pointed look but Hetty was too distraught to respond with anything more than another truncated sob.

She did not care that they must guess at the cause of her distress when she raced up the steps once they reached their townhouse.

The butler was slow in opening the door and as she waited, she heard Stephen ask Araminta, clearly bemused, "She can't possibly be in love with the fellow, can she? I thought she barely knew him."

Then Araminta's thoughtful response, "Perhaps Hetty has more secrets than we realized."

Chapter Nine

Hetty was lying on her bed later that evening when her mother quietly entered the room.

"My poor darling," she said, taking a seat by Hetty's side and filling her with the comfort Hetty always felt at her mother's lavender-scented presence. "Araminta said you were feeling poorly and suggested I see what I could do for you."

"I doubt the concern came from Araminta," muttered Hetty, enjoying the gentle hand massage her mother was giving her. "What did she really tell you?"

"Well, to be honest, she said it appeared you'd lost your head over some unsuitable rogue. I, however, would suggest you've lost your heart. You never were in danger of losing your head. It's far too sensibly screwed on."

Hetty closed her eyes and said miserably, "Not in this instance. Araminta's right. I have lost my head and my heart and no doubt I'll suffer for it the rest of my life."

"Come, my darling, it can't be that terrible. Not if you barely know the gentleman as Araminta says." Lady Partington's tone hardened. "Sir Aubrey would not be my choice of husband for you, Hetty. Stephen doesn't think at all highly of him."

"And why should Stephen's opinion count for more than mine?" Hetty sniffed. "If he told you Sir Aubrey was the best candidate a girl could hope for you'd be counseling me very differently. All these unfounded rumors." She drew in a shaky breath. "I only wish the truth were known."

"Really, Hetty darling." Her mother sounded put out. "Cousin Stephen works in the Foreign Office so of course he knows things we can't possibly be expected to know. We have to take his opinion when it's offered. Now come along, my love, and drink this. Martha has just warmed it and it'll make you feel much more the thing."

Grumbling like the child she'd so recently been, Hetty

allowed her mother to help her into a sitting position before taking the fragrant milk. It was hard to attend to these well-meaning platitudes when all she could think about was how she was going to disprove the rumors everyone insisted precluded Sir Aubrey from being an acceptable suitor. Not that he was going to marry her.

Nevertheless, she would be the one responsible for removing the tarnish that blackened his name. He might not thank her for it in the way she wished, but the thought of it made her feel strong and powerful.

* * *

After a great deal of tossing and turning and soul-searching during the night, Hetty felt much better. She could accept now that while she was not the bride Sir Aubrey would choose, she could at least be responsible for advancing his happiness and good fortune. Advancing other people's happiness had always given her pleasure.

In this lighter, virtuous frame of mind, she went riding with Stephen in the morning, attending to him with all the cheeriness of her old self so that he remarked, "Well, my dear, I'm glad your sister's pronouncements regarding your foolishness turned out to be so off the mark."

"I suppose you mean Sir Aubrey." Hetty slanted a disgusted look at her cousin. "Araminta thinks Mr. Woking is my perfect match."

Stephen matched her grimace. "My dear girl, I regard any relation of Lord Debenham with as much enthusiasm as I do Sir Aubrey. Lord Debenham might not be in the same sinister league as your friend Sir Aubrey but he has a reputation for debauchery nonetheless. I'd much prefer to see you wed someone kind and gentle who'd appreciate your quiet charm as much as your sister is admired by the more adventurous for her dazzling attributes."

Later that day, when Jane was brushing her hair, Hetty announced she needed her maid to accompany her on a shopping expedition for a new pair of York tan gloves. It was only when they were in the carriage that she leaned across to reveal the real motivation for their journey. Wanting to make amends to Jane was part of it.

"I know you were cross with me for saying anything to your young man but the fact is we're about to visit him now. He's promised I can view the letter in his possession." At Jane's horrified gasp, Hetty added quickly, "You mustn't worry, Jane, for this will all end very well." She truly did believe that. "Yes, it was wrong of Jem to take the letter but it was a good thing, otherwise Lord Debenham would have destroyed it. I'm certain that once I read its contents I will know how to use it to exonerate Sir Aubrey."

Jane's eyes grew large. "Jem is expecting you?" She shook her head. "Oh miss, I thought he was expecting Miss Araminta."

"And why my sister when she knows nothing of this?"

Jane twisted her hands in her lap while a kernel of doubt lodged in Hetty's breast.

"Miss Araminta quizzed me this mornin'," said Jane. "Sounded as if she knew all about it, she did. Said, in fact, you'd asked for her help as you were afraid of goin' after the letter alone and that she'd agreed she would see Jem and discover if there were anything to the whole business."

Hetty's mouth dropped open. Her brain grasped for the true meaning in all this.

Jane looked more distressed than ever. "I didn't know it were a secret and…I dunno but I might of said something I shouldna."

The familiar impotent rage Hetty always felt when her sister walked roughshod over her hopes and dreams threatened to sweep her away like a tidal wave. Araminta was yet again one step ahead. Hetty, the quiet and meek little sister everyone overlooked, could never keep up. Didn't this just prove it? While Hetty had done all the hard work and set the stage for triumph, Araminta was going to reap the prize.

* * *

Tears pricked her eyelids as she sank back against the squabs and surrendered to the jolting motion of the carriage ride.

"Miss, are you all right?" Jane sounded anxious. "We'll still visit my Jem, won't we? After all, we want to know what Miss Araminta plans to do next, don't we?"

Little matter if Jane's preoccupation was with seeing her young man.

Wearily, Hetty ran the back of her hand across her heated brow. "Yes, Jane, we'll still see Jem. Araminta might have read the letter and told him it contained nothing of any account."

Her earlier anticipation turned leaden as she stepped out of the carriage. She patted the floral festooned bonnet she wore, a ridiculous piece of frippery she'd chosen specially for her intended triumphant progress from visiting Jem to seeing Sir Aubrey. Her heart shriveled inside her chest.

She should be used to being left behind. Perhaps it was all over for her already. Perhaps at this very moment Sir Aubrey was in possession of a special license in anticipation of Araminta's triumph and when Hetty returned home, Araminta would ask her to be maid of honor. That is, if she wasn't married to him already.

When Jem arrived at the designated coffeehouse, he slipped into a booth, barely looking either of the young women in the eye.

"Dunno why you sent your sister when you're here anyways," he muttered. "The fewer what knows, the better, I say."

There was no purpose in telling Jem the truth. Hetty got to the point. "What did my sister say when she saw the letter?"

"That I'd be rewarded handsomely. Miss Partington has a glib tongue on her, I'll give her that."

"You should never have taken that letter, Jem," Jane burst out. She reached out her thin hands across the worn wooden tabletop in a gesture of angry despair. "I jes hope you ain't going to rot in a cell for it."

Hetty closed her eyes briefly, almost too fearful to ask the question. For if Araminta had made off with it, there was nothing Hetty could do. "Where is the letter, Jem?"

"I ain't got it with me. Put it back, didn't I, after Miss Partington saw it." He raked his hand through his straw-colored hair, wearing the expression of one who has just about reached the end of his tether.

Hope flickered in Hetty's breast. "She didn't take it?"

"Said she didn't have the money but she knew someone who did and that she'd come back."

Hetty's heart pounded painfully as she leaned forward. "When did she leave? Do you know where she went? And when can I see the letter?"

He sent her a wry look. "Miss Araminta left less than a half hour ago and I'd only just hid the letter again and was back at me work when I heard you was wantin' to see me after all."

"Please, Jem, I have to see that letter." Hetty knew she sounded desperate. "I'll pay you well for it, I promise."

"Ain't worth me job to fetch it back again now. Me master'll be comin' back from his ride and I got to get 'im ready. As for your sister, I dunno where she went." He nodded his indication the interview was at an end. "With respect, miss, let me tells yer this, I'll be givin' that letter to the first person what gives me a fiver fer it."

"That's downright greedy, Jem," Jane sniffed. "You're just lucky you are that Miss Hetty ain't about to turn you in."

"Reckon it's a sore point wiv me that someone else turned me in already," he said with a pointed look at Jane.

Hetty rose quickly. There was no time for recriminations when her greatest priority was to find Araminta. Perhaps she'd written down the words or committed them to memory and was now on her way to find Sir Aubrey.

A final question struck Hetty as she turned to leave. "Who was with her? She couldn't have come alone."

Jem shrugged. "Reckoned it were Miss Partington's sister 'til I saw that Miss Lissa—that were her name—were dressed shabby, like a governess or summat."

"What!" Hetty swung around. "A young woman who looked like Araminta's sister? It's not possible. We have no relatives in London." But already an uncomfortable thought had taken root. Once again, there were those odd pieces of the family puzzle she'd only just begun to piece together. She squeezed her eyes shut quickly, not wanting to visit the uncomfortable subject she'd heard whispered about over the years. Six months ago it would have seemed impossible that her dear, loyal papa had no other children. But her safe and ordered life seemed to have been turned on its head since then. She fisted her hands and said, "Come, Jane, we must hurry home and find Araminta." She didn't want to think about who this Miss Lissa was to her. Or Araminta.

"We must get them gloves on the way, miss, else Lady Partington will ask questions."

"Just quickly, then," Hetty acceded reluctantly, knowing how much her maid liked to browse at all the pretty things the shopkeepers showed them.

Mixed fortune came their way when they stepped into Hetty's favorite glove makers on Bond Street. A lady who had her back to them as she scrutinized a selection of finely stitched gloves turned at their arrival, and Hetty found herself face- to-face with the golden-haired, duplicitous creature she despised more than any other and whom she'd hoped never to set eyes on again.

"Why, Miss Henrietta, I barely recognized you!" exclaimed

Lady Julia, brazen as ever, for no blush of shame swept her cheeks as she greeted Hetty with every apparent pleasure.

Hetty could hardly believe it. Lady Julia, the faithless *married* swine who'd taken Cousin Edgar on his final boating jaunt before he drowned six months ago appeared to harbor no guilt at all. She was smiling as if recalling fond past pleasures.

All Hetty could recall as she stared back was the pain of seeing her beloved cousin writhing in passion in the scheming minx's arms before the drunken pair had fallen out of their boat in the dam at The Grange.

"Indeed, Miss Henrietta, you are *greatly* improved in looks. And how is your cousin?"

For one shocked moment Hetty thought Lady Julia referred to Edgar. She bit back the retort that of course he was being looked after by the angels, thanks to Lady Julia's wickedness. "I presume you mean Cousin Stephen?"

"Of course I do." Lady Julia's tinkling laugh rang out as she patted her swollen belly. "He and I are old friends, you know. He was a guest of my husband's just before he took up residence at The Grange. You were just a child back then, it seemed. But now you're a grown woman. Do tell him the child is due in November. He'll want to know, I'm sure."

Hetty's brow crinkled in confusion. But instead of questioning her, she merely nodded her head once while her gaze returned to the woman's extended belly. Why, she looked even larger than Hetty's mama who'd declared she was far too advanced to be seen out in public.

Hetty was irked beyond measure that Lady Julia looked so blooming. Her flaxen hair was demurely arranged beneath a becoming floral-festooned bonnet that made Hetty feel hers was vastly overdone. Lady Julia, like Araminta, had always put her in the shade.

"I'll pass on your greeting," she muttered finally, tugging Jane's sleeve as she turned to leave but Lady's Julia's laughing response gave her pause.

"You're a great deal more gracious than your sister, Miss Henrietta, for when she stepped in here when I was perusing some fine evening gloves earlier, she gave me the cut direct."

Hetty swung back from the doorway. "Araminta was here?"

"With her poor relation, by the look of it."

Hetty hurried back to their townhouse, but though it was late in the afternoon, her sister was not at home. "Gone on the promenade," said Betty, who attended their mother and had come down from The Grange. "No doubt with that gentlemen she's got her sights set on though she said she had another errand she had to attend to quickly, first. Mr Cranbourne said the invitation to go walking was no longer on the table, but if Miss Araminta has a mind to do something—"

Hetty didn't wait to hear more. When she burst into her mother's room and questioned her on Araminta's movements, Lady Partington raised her hands, palms upwards. "Araminta insisted that these rumours that surround Sir Aubrey are quite unsubstantiated but that she wouldn't go walking with him, if it made me unhappy. Now you're telling me she's not here?"

Hetty could not, of course, probe further as to what she knew of Hetty's companion.

It was a different matter with her father. He studied her silently over the top of his news sheet when she found him in his study. "A young lady who looks so like your sister as to be remarked upon? *Here?*" He harrumphed as his eyes flicked from Hetty's face back to the news sheet. "I don't know what you're talking about, my dear."

Clearly he'd long since decided silence and obfuscation were the only ways to deal with potentially awkward situations like this. Defeated, Hetty returned to her room where she paced up and down, chewing her fingernails and wondering what to do.

Araminta would be visiting Sir Aubrey with details about the letter Jem had in his possession. The letter that *Hetty* had ferreted out! Yet she hadn't had the money to pay Jem for it when she'd seen him earlier that morning. Had she rushed back to get sufficient funds and perhaps only just left the house with no one seeing her, intent upon meeting Jem again before travelling onwards to present Sir Aubrey with it?

After some minutes pondering the dilemma of what to do next, Hetty became aware of a figure standing on the pavement beneath a plane tree on the other side of the road. The young woman's poke bonnet concealed her face but her figure and dress proclaimed her of middling rank and perhaps around Hetty's age.

Hetty went to the sash window and peered out. The movement immediately drew the attention of the young person who raised her head and gave a surreptitious wave.

Pushing up the window, Hetty put her head out and squinted. A passing carriage obscured the figure and when it had passed, the girl was gone. Then Hetty realized she was crossing the road, indicating for Hetty to meet her at the railing beside the portico.

Snatching a shawl, Hetty hurried down the stairs and emerged onto the pavement, saying without preamble, "You know where Araminta has gone, don't you? You were with her earlier."

The young woman nodded. She bore a greater resemblance to her sister than Hetty had at first thought, though her expression had a more serious cast to it. The well- shaped nose and brow, the full upper lip and the arched brows above flashing green eyes were, however, clearly from the same mold.

"Why were you with Araminta? And who are you?" The questions tumbled out as Hetty remembered seeing this girl in the village church though she'd not remarked upon any particular resemblance at the time. She'd been younger then, so perhaps her features had not matured.

"My name is Larissa and I met your sister by chance when she first came to London a few weeks ago. Today, to my surprise, she sent a note around asking me to accompany her to a secret meeting in a coffeehouse." The girl's expression gave nothing away. "I'm a governess and my young charge is being fitted for a new gown. As she's going in company with her mama, I was spared the ordeal." Only her lips stretched into something resembling a wry smile. "Miss Araminta said I was to keep the visit secret and it was my intention to simply return to the household where I'm presently employed...only I was concerned."

Hetty trembled. This was confirmation of her own fears. Fears that Araminta was about to ruin Hetty's carefully orchestrated plan and win Sir Aubrey through such underhanded and underserving means.

Hetty thrust out her chin. "Well, I've just seen the young valet, Jem. Araminta was seeing him about a letter. You know that, obviously. Well, since he's told me he still had the letter because Araminta didn't have the funds to pay him what he wanted, I expect she's returned secretly."

She knew she sounded childish and aggrieved. She had little doubt that Larissa had been briefed by Araminta on the reason they were going to see Jem otherwise why was she here?

"So Miss Araminta has not returned home?"

"No." Hetty looked at her oddly, then asked, "And why were you standing there, watching the house, if you only recently returned here with my sister? Is there something else you want to tell me?" This was all very strange. Jem still had the letter and if Araminta wasn't at home now, it *must* be because she was back seeing Jem. Hetty must have just missed her!

"I didn't return with your sister."

Hetty frowned. She wondered if the girl was here for money. She didn't look avaricious sort. She held herself with a kind of brittle pride. As if she were reluctant to have anything to do with Hetty, in fact, which was rich considering Hetty had every right to despise this ill-begotten child of...her father's.

She clapped her hands to her mouth as the shaming thought entered her mind.

But immediately her concerns regarding Araminta took precedence. Was her sister in some danger? Was *that* why this young woman was here? Abruptly, she asked, "If Araminta didn't accompany you here, where is she now and what are you doing here?"

Larissa shrugged. "I wasn't going to approach you. I shouldn't, that is. But, as I said, I was concerned—"

"Concerned? About my sister's safety? I think Araminta can look after herself very nicely. No doubt she's already slipped away with the letter to give it to Sir Aubrey. I'll wager that's where she is right now!" Blinding anger came crashing down upon Hetty's shoulders as she considered this as the only likely scenario but the governess shook her head.

"No, I don't think so. You see, I was with your sister when the footman showed her the letter and —"

Dully, Hetty interrupted. "What was her reaction when she read it?"

"Something along the lines of: 'Oh my goodness, what a delightful shock! Sir Aubrey will be so pleased with me!'"

Hetty felt like screaming. Then a sudden thought occurred to her. "Jem said Araminta didn't take it but she *did*, didn't she? She paid him to tell me a lie to throw me off the scent and now she's not gone to see Jem, she's taken the letter to Sir Aubrey, herself!"

She knew she was overwrought because the self-contained creature widened her eyes as she stepped back, saying, "No, nothing like that! The reason I'm here is that your sister requested I chaperone her to her meeting place. She had no one else she could ask, she told me. But then she disappeared when we were leaving the tavern." Briefly, Larissa put her hands to her face and when she dropped them she looked pale and worried. "The truth is, I care little for your sister but I knew Pa— I mean, her father would be furious is she were discovered missing, especially if he learned I was the last person to see her." She glanced at the sky. "It's getting late you see, and Miss Araminta just vanished."

For the first time a kernel of worry for Araminta manifested itself in Hetty's breast. "Did Jem turn nasty?" she asked on a frightened whisper. "Could he have done something?"

The girl hushed her alarm. "It's true he was mighty cross when she snatched the letter, only he took it back and then Miss Araminta jumped up and flounced through the room, with everyone looking at her as she said over her shoulder that she reckoned a fine lady would be believed over a mere footman, and to consider himself lucky that he wasn't going to swing."

"But you must have followed Araminta. Where did she go? Where is she now?"

Larissa looked helpless. "I can't tell you. I followed her, of course, but when I stepped onto the pavement she was nowhere to be seen." She bit her lip. "I thought it was very odd that she'd leave, unaccompanied, much less leave me there alone, but she'd been in high dudgeon and I've observed her over the years, so perhaps it wasn't so surprising."

Hetty made no remark to this acute observation. In fact, she tried to cast it from her mind. She was not ready for her recent suspicions to be so irrefutably confirmed. "How long have you been waiting here and if you were concerned, why didn't you make yourself known earlier?"

A blush swept the girl's pale cheeks. "I was instructed never to make myself known here."

"You could have sent a message," Hetty muttered. "You could have given it to someone in the kitchen."

Larissa shook her head. "There's some who know me and they'd report it. Lord Partington would be incensed if he knew I'd had anything to do with any of his…daughters." She glanced up at the windows of the four square house then back at Hetty. "I must return to my employer. I hope Miss Araminta is safe. I've told you everything I know."

There was no point in trying to detain the girl. Nor to question her further, for it was quite clear Larissa the governess was Lord Partington's daughter. Hetty digested this painfully as she watched the girl leave, her serviceable boots showing cracked and worn beneath the hem of her dull, plain skirt. She'd thought she'd hate her, this girl who represented her father's failings and her mother's unhappiness. Until recently, Hetty had been able to bury her head in the sand and pretend ignorance of life's painful realities. Now she understood the dangers too clearly to do nothing.

She cast another worried look at the sky. It would soon be dusk. The long summer twilight was in her favor but Hetty's hands were tied. What could she, a single, innocent female, do to solve a mystery she wasn't even sure was a mystery? What if Araminta had done exactly as Hetty had done? Assumed subterfuge to indulge her fascination for a gentleman she was being warned off?

The thought that right now Araminta was with Sir Aubrey, giving him the letter his late wife had written, made Hetty feel ill as she trod the back stairs to her bedchamber.

And what would be her reward? Was Araminta at this moment wrapped in the arms of the man who had been Hetty's lover?

Regardless of propriety and the inherent danger, she had to find out.

Chapter Ten

SIR AUBREY STRETCHED out his long legs as he savored the last of his cheroot before tossing it into the fire. There was little else to savor these days, he thought sourly.

He reached for the decanter at his elbow and shakily poured himself another measure of whisky.

Since depositing that alluring, too-innocent-for-anyone miss with her cousin and older sister after their phaeton ride, he'd felt as if the sun had gone out of his life.

"Leave it!" he snapped to the unwary parlor maid who, clearly not realizing he was in the room, had drawn the curtains, highlighting the fact that everything bright and joyous was beyond his library and out of reach.

Out of reach. His Henrietta would be forever out of reach. She had taken far too bold a risk for one in her position and she'd singed her wings and come crashing down to cold, base reality. She now must realize there was nothing he could or would do.

Unless, of course, there were consequences, though he'd been careful, as always. When he took a wife it would be to further his own comfort and to sire an heir, but never would he willingly sire a bastard.

He only prayed to God there would be no inconvenient repercussions so Miss Henrietta Partington would be spared an unfit husband such as himself. He was prepared to do as honor required but fortunately she had seen fit to realize she would never have his heart; that she had put herself forever out of his reach.

He was roused from his torpid languor by a rapping on the library door, which was pushed open by the recently dismissed housemaid. The cheery smile she'd turned upon him when he interrupted her earlier was replaced by a look bordering on trepidation. Good. Women should be afraid of him. He was not a nice man. Only if his appetites for the fine life were indulged was he prepared to show his more charming side. Margaret had said it.

She'd cited it as a reason for leaving him—the fact he was not the sunny-tempered charmer she claimed her cousin Lord Debenham was.

Well, Debenham was the least sunny-tempered gentleman of his acquaintance but clearly he knew how to put on a good show. Sir Aubrey did not believe in dressing up the truth. If he felt out of sorts, he'd take himself off elsewhere until his mood had passed. He was not given to playacting.

Unlike the deceiving wench Miss Henrietta Partington, who clearly was nothing like he'd believed. He had a deep-rooted contempt for deception. Margaret had deceived him. She had received him with pretended pleasure but she had deceived him into imagining that he was pleasing to his delicate wife.

And now, if Miss Henrietta hadn't already taken deception to the greatest heights possible for a young woman in her position, surely she'd gone one step further, he thought with horror as she was shown in. Despite the heavy veiling, it could be none other.

Come to persuade him to alter his mind and...what? Marry her? Take her to bed?

He narrowed his eyes as he prepared his defenses, trying to armor himself against the arousal her clasped hands and trembling form unleashed in him. For although he could see nothing of her face, he could well imagine her soft brown eyes appealing to him from her pretty round face, an affecting performance enhanced by a suitably trembling lower lip. How he longed to nip that lip and how fiercely he had to rein in his desire.

"I cannot possibly receive you, Miss Partington," he said in a voice intended to repulse her with its lack of warmth. "You are unaccompanied." He hated himself as much as he longed for her.

"Where is Araminta?" she burst out.

He had not expected this. She was halfway across the room, her eyes boring into him with real concern now that she'd raised her veil.

Forcing distance into his tone, a feeling he was so far from experiencing as to be laughable, he strolled to the window and stared into the street.

"Why, you are more of a play actress than I'd have given you credit for, Miss Henrietta. You do the profession proud."

It was close to a direct insult and he expected she'd take grave offense. Instead she covered her hands with her mouth as she gasped, "So she really isn't here with you?"

He couldn't tell if she was more upset or relieved. Certainly both registered in the look she sent him and the way she sank against the back of the sofa.

With a sense of righteous indignation, he went on. "Did you imagine I followed up our phaeton ride with the type of assignation I've enjoyed with you, Miss Henrietta? Why, that notion seems to upset you. Don't forget, my dear, you pretended to be someone who'd entered a profession not known for its discernment. A business transaction that takes no account of the heart."

He told himself he didn't care that she looked as if he'd shredded her heart in two. Hadn't she done the same to him?

"I would never have given myself to any other man!" Her lips were tightly pressed together, her eyes wild as they bored into him. "I told you the reasons. But perhaps I was too glad of an excuse to give myself to you when you were the only man I had…any little bit of feeling for."

"And so that might have been…at the start," Sir Aubrey muttered, thinking of how appealing she'd appeared when he'd first taken her, trembling but oh so eager, into his embrace. "What about your feelings for Lord Debenham? I found you in his arms, too, don't forget." He knew he was being unfair but he had to make her hate him.

"If you are so off the mark as regards feelings for Lord Debenham then you have absolutely no idea what danger my sister could be in." The vulnerable maiden had given way to the vengeful siren. She looked ready to claw his eyes out. "You think I'd go willingly to your…enemy? Why, I…I abhor the man!" She took what she assumed were meant to be menacing steps toward him while he stood his ground, willing her to give up the fight at the same time as hoping she'd hurl herself into his arms.

He shrugged. "What am I to think? Disciples of Venus do not seek out men they love." He snorted the word with derision. It felt good; but only for a moment. "When you threw yourself at me with such feeling after I supposedly rescued you from Debenham, I was quite touched. I certainly was not suspicious."

"Suspicious?" She looked at him askance. "I told you the truth when I said he attacked me. Are you really unaware of my feelings and what I've been trying to do for you?"

He laughed out loud at this. "My avenging little angel, are

you, Miss Henrietta Partington, daughter of a viscount and cousin to a man who has accepted conventional wisdom that I am a villain? Oh, I've heard it all. The whispers that I'm a wife-beater, a man who chased Margaret into the arms of another when my brutality could no longer be borne. There's worse, of course, and I had, until recently, assumed you would know nothing of that, however your cozy association with Lord Debenham has persuaded me otherwise."

She looked confused but poised for attack.

"Now that I see what circles you frequent, I understand how very useful you might be to those enemies of mine who are trying to secure the evidence needed to convict me of crimes of which the court of gossip long since convicted me." He realized he'd gone too far. What would she know of sordid politics? He did not really believe her involved in anything other than a deception she'd carried too far.

Nevertheless, she nodded. "The Castlereagh affair. Some think you a Spencean. That you should swing."

His initial surprise turned to disappointment. "So you're well versed in the story, are you? That's what you were looking for when I discovered you in my bedchamber, isn't it? Evidence to convict me. You'd been sent by your cousin, or perhaps Lord Debenham." He gave a short laugh to hide his devastation as he pretended preoccupation with the crisp crease of his coat cuff, unable to bear the sight of her pretended innocent horror. "You were so terrified I truly was guilty you sacrificed your virtue, thinking I might take your life. Well, the joke is on you, Miss Henrietta, because you will find no evidence. You sacrificed your virtue for nothing."

"That's not true!" she cried, rushing forward, and for one gloriously confusing moment he believed she really was going to throw herself into his embrace. How much easier it would be to proceed if the passion were elevated. They were well matched. Or so he had thought.

Bitterly he realized now it had all been to secure what she and her cohorts believed he had—evidence that would convict him of an illegal association of which he was innocent. Now once again she was trying to play him for a fool.

"I admired you from afar and then...I loved you." She sniffed. "I still do. I did not sacrifice anything I was not at least secretly willing to give. But now Araminta has taken it upon herself to do what I had intended on your behalf and she has disappeared." She glanced toward the window. "The day is closing in and I need to find her before a terrible scandal possibly erupts. That's why I'm here."

"To find Araminta? My dear," he shook his head, "your sister holds even less interest for me than you do. So please, suspend all this dramatic talk about what you'd intended on my behalf. The kindest thing you can do for me right now is simply to pull down that hideous veil and take yourself off to your comfortable home and never trouble me again."

"Araminta has disappeared and if she's not with you, I fear she's with Lord Debenham."

"Doing what you failed to do, my dear?"

She shook her head wildly. "No! Will you please listen to me without all these snide interjections that make me realize you have absolutely no idea what is going on and who is in jeopardy as a result?"

For the first time, a kernel of doubt crept into his skeptical mind.

She put her hands to her face and in agitation began to pace. "It so happens," she said, "that my lady's maid is sweetheart to Lord Debenham's valet. I had no idea of this until two nights ago when she told me a secret the young man had told her." Miss Henrietta swung around in orange-water-scented dudgeon. "It was about a letter he had taken, written by your late wife, which he had found in Lord Debenham's library."

He felt the blood drain from his head and reached for the mantelpiece to steady himself. Was she laughing at him?

No, it appeared she really was serious.

"Margaret *really* wrote a letter?" he whispered. "And it has been *found*?"

Miss Henrietta nodded. Her expression softened and when she placed a tentative hand on his coat sleeve he did not shake it off.

With difficulty he asked, for he feared the answer would not be one he wanted, "To whom did she write it? What does it say?"

"I do not know." She gave a frustrated sigh. "The letter disappeared but at least the mystery as to who possesses it has been solved. Lord Debenham's valet Jem took it but he cannot read. He simply assumed it contained things Lord Debenham wouldn't want made public and he's been using it as blackmail against his master. The fact Lord Debenham is afraid of it being made public is borne up by the fact that Jem has kept his job, and it appears Lord Debenham is careful to keep the young man onside."

Sir Aubrey, wishing Miss Henrietta was still gripping his sleeve, stroked his chin thoughtfully. "Well, it can't have contained anything of any moment if this lad has simply kept the letter and did nothing."

The little minx now put her head on one side and smiled. "Jem is a very handsome young man but I do not think he is particularly clever or cunning." She almost spoke to him as if she felt he, too, could be similarly categorized. "For a start, he knew he'd done something wrong in taking the letter—"

"Damn right he did! How did he come by it? If he took it from Margaret's...body...then it's a hanging offense."

"My maid says her young man stole it from Debenham after he foolishly fell asleep with the letter beside him."

He looked at her, impressed. She really had done her research.

Hetty nodded as she went on. "Since he couldn't read he pocketed it, hoping to secure his own livelihood as valet to Lord Debenham."

"So he has kept this letter? Hidden and unread for nearly two years?"

Miss Henrietta nodded. "It would appear so."

"Then how has your sister become involved in all this? She doesn't appear the sleuth you are, Miss Henrietta...about whom I am now beginning to feel more favorably."

She graced him with a beatific smile. "That's good, for my motivation in all this has been to make you beholden to me."

"So I would marry you?" He turned away, though not before he saw the flicker of dismay that crossed her face.

She thrust out her chin as she moved in front of him. "I never expected that." Her voice shook. "I never expected to make a match that would please me, so I certainly never expected you would look twice at me. And I was proved right, for you danced many times with Araminta but never with me."

"I never saw you!"

"No one ever sees me beside Araminta. She's the beauty of the family. Beside her I'm a pale, dreary wallflower. Then, when I fell into danger with you, I was suddenly presented with an offer I couldn't refuse. Oh, I knew that I was going to burn in hell for my sins and that you thought you were paying me but that was better, I believed, than marrying Mr. Woking."

He shuddered. "Mr. Roderick Woking. Good god, yes! So you're telling me you chose sin and pleasure with me over respectable marriage with Mr. Woking?" He gave her a wry smile. "I think most ladies would have."

"This is no time for funning!"

"My apologies," he murmured, resisting the urge to put a conciliatory arm about her shoulders for fear it would lead to more than he was prepared to risk. "However I think we're straying off the most important subject at hand, and that is how your sister came to be involved."

"Yes! And I'm worried about her! She took my place when she learned I was to meet Jem at a secret location. He showed her the letter. Then, according to her companion, she disappeared between leaving the booth where they were talking, and the street."

"Very curious, as is the fact that I'm the last to know of a letter stolen from my late wife." He looked at her darkly. "I hope this is not a competition between two sisters for my affections, to see who can restore the letter to me first and so win my hand?"

She had the grace to blush while a curious emotion churned within him. This, to all intents, virtuous young lady had risked everything for a few moments of pleasure. Then when exposure appeared likely, she pounced upon a means to clear his name so that he would reward her with...his.

Yes, he was suspicious. The sudden appearance of this letter was too convenient. Miss Henrietta was clearly the mistress of subterfuge despite her innocent looks. The more he considered the thought, the more it seemed plausible that she had invented the whole thing and the letter would prove a forgery. Likely as not, she was here on the pretext of a missing sister, to urge him into the drama and so achieve her ends—his eternal gratitude.

Nevertheless, if a letter existed, and whether it was a forgery or not, he had to had to find out.

* * *

Araminta pulled the hood of her dark cloak farther down her

face and hunched her shoulders while she waited for Lord Debenham to issue out of his club. Hopefully he'd choose to walk the short distance to his home rather than take his carriage. She shivered, as much from apprehension as excitement, for an unmarried young woman courted ruin if she were to be seen approaching a gentleman in this manner. She should never be here, of course, but the idea had only occurred to her as she'd left the coffee house with Lissa from whom she had, for a moment, become separated. When she'd turned to see Jem, alone and watching her, she'd made the most daring and impulsive decision of her life.

Waiting for Lord Debenham, now, was the second.

What it was to have choices! As a closely guarded young woman she'd been able to make very few of those. She'd almost envied Lissa's ability to be able to walk, unchaperoned, the few blocks from where she worked as a governess to answer Araminta's summons earlier that day—though of course Araminta wouldn't ever sacrifice status for freedom.

However, as the wife of a peer of the realm, she'd have both.

And the knowledge of what the letter Jem had stolen contained gave her more power than she could have believed.

She caught her breath and kept, for the moment, within the shadows of the row of buildings behind her. There he was. No one could mistake his tall, sartorial elegance, his glossy, raven hair revealed a moment before he replaced his hat, his long legs encased in fashionable trousers. A contrasting image of Sir Aubrey flitted across her mind. He was more classically handsome and, yes, far less dangerous now she knew the truth, yet Sir Aubrey did not possess the landholdings Lord Debenham did.

And there was the title, of course.

"Lord Debenham, I must speak with you!" She stepped out of the shadows and into his path raising her veil to catch a glimpse of his shocked face when he realized her identity but forestalled him, saying, "A hackney is just passing. Please help me in. What I have to say will only take a minute."

He acceded to her request but appeared angry as he faced her across the dim interior after ordering the harvey to drive around the park until further notice. "What kind of ruse is this, Miss Partington? If we were discovered your reputation would be in tatters and I would be called upon to do the honorable thing."

"Your reputation is about to be in tatters and it is I who am doing the honorable thing." She smiled, thinking herself rather clever to have delivered such a line.

It certainly made its mark, for he narrowed his eyes and muttered, "Well, then?"

She gave a deep sigh. "Lord Debenham, I have long admired you, not least for your integrity."

"What is this, Miss Partington? A rehearsed speech? Has someone put you up to this? Am I about to be blackmailed?"

Crossly she said, "Well, it did take rather a long time to learn that line off by heart but as to being blackmailed, you certainly will be if what I'm about to tell you becomes known in public circles."

His face contorted for a moment before, in a low voice, he asked, "What are you talking about?"

There. Now he was paying her the attention he ought.

Demurely, she clasped her hands in her lap and dropped her eyes. "It concerns a certain letter, Lord Debenham."

Venturing a glance at his face in the lengthening silence, she saw both fear and suspicion as he muttered, "What letter is this?

"The letter your valet Jem has in his possession."

She was unprepared for his sudden movement. It was as if he had been mortally wounded, the way he jerked back against the squabs.

"It exists?"

Araminta nodded. "I saw it just half an hour ago. Apparently when my sister learned of its existence, she made an arrangement with your valet to look at it. My sister, it transpires, has lost her heart to Sir Aubrey and I believe it was her intention to take the letter to him."

She saw as they passed beneath a street lamp that he'd gone a rather pallid, greyish color. Yes, he was definitely taking notice of her, now. Raking a hand through his hair, he whispered, "Who, other than you, has read that letter and where is it now?"

"I'm the only one, Lord Debenham, and Jem has the letter since he wouldn't give it to me, despite all my inducements."

"What inducements were those, might I ask?"

"He wanted two guineas for it but unfortunately I had only half a crown. Apparently you never offered him a groat."

He uttered an expletive she clearly wasn't intended to hear. Then, "So you're blackmailing me, Miss Partington? Perhaps you and this valet of mine? He says I never offered him a groat? Ha! He only ever hinted at knowing more about matters than might be desirable. He was obviously frightened, knowing I'd have the law on my side if he were found guilty of stealing."

Araminta widened her eyes. "Good gracious, my lord, I only want to help you! It was very unfortunate I didn't have more to offer your man and so be able to hand over the letter to you now. You really would want to have it as Lady Margaret says terrible things about you. However, I am simply an unworldly debutante." She sent him a knowing look and went on with a sigh, "Hoping to make a good match. As I said, I've long admired you, Lord Debenham." She lowered her eyes.

Initially he did not respond as she'd expected. After a long, tense silence, he leaned forward and clasped one of her hands. "Clearly you are a young lady who thrives on risk," His voice was soft. Ah, that was better.

For a moment she thought he might brush her lips with his and wasn't sure if she was relieved or disappointed he did not. She'd been attracted to him when she first had met him but subsequent tales of his exploits had been more than concerning. Nevertheless, her confidence was in the ascendant now. She knew that successful handling of a gentleman could be managed by allure, which she possessed in abundance. Sir Aubrey had been perfectly hateful to her during their phaeton ride but perhaps Lord Debenham, with his veneer of danger, was someone she *could* tame. She liked a challenge and the fact was, he *did* come with a title. The way he was reacting now certainly suggested she had him in the palm of her hand.

"Do you recall what else it mentioned, Miss Partington?"

Araminta felt a trifle nervous at the intensity of his look but managed a bold smile. "Only about your club, my Lord."

He raised his eyebrows. "My club?"

"The Spencean Club."

She wasn't sure if she imagined it, the dangerous flash in his eyes, for suddenly he relaxed back against the squabs and said, almost genially, "I trust you can insinuate your way back inside your home and keep silent about this afternoon's activities." Then his expression took on a most intimate and intense look as he added with exciting portent, "That is, if there is to be a desirable outcome from our little interview."

Nevertheless, Araminta wasn't sure Lord Debenham had been suitably grateful. When she looked at him again, he was gazing at the ceiling as if she didn't exist. "If that's all the thanks I get, Lord Debenham—" she began but he cut her off.

"I did not mean to make you angry." His attention was fully upon her now. She noticed his breathing was rather rapid and his eyes looked fevered.

Good, she thought again, satisfied that the promise of her affections was finally having the desired effect.

"It is a rare opportunity to be in such close proximity to a lady." He swallowed. "A potential savior. You have been very good to me and I intend to reward you as you deserve. May I be so bold as to beg a kiss?"

She felt like the cat who had swallowed the cream, raising her face delicately to his and saying, "It is a great risk we take, Lord Debenham, for if we are caught the consequences would be very dire."

Already he was closing in on her, his arms wrapping about her shoulders, his breath tickling her ear. She shuddered at the extraordinary responses of her body and part of her realized the element of danger was an aphrodisiac in itself. She'd never felt this roiling in her lower belly or the heightened sensitivity of her skin as he caressed her cheek with his lips.

"I might have to offer to marry you, Miss Partington," he whispered, touching his lips to hers.

She let out her breath in a satisfied sigh, surrendering to the strange sensations that enveloped her, disappointed when he set her away from him and reached over to open the door.

But his parting words as he raised her hand for his kiss were just what she was after. "I shall let you off at the park as it certainly wouldn't do for you to be discovered alone with me, outside your home. However, if I were called upon to do as honor dictated it would not be a hardship, Miss Partington."

Just before he closed the door between them, he slipped a five-pound note into her hand. "If you can get that letter for me, I will ensure that you are appropriately rewarded. But let us not part when we have no plans to meet again. What say you this evening, at Lady Scott's ball? I know the house well. There is a door hidden behind the tapestry on the rear saloon wall. Impossible to miss if you know what you're looking for. On the stroke of midnight I will be waiting in the withdrawing room. It is the second door on the corridor at right angles to the ladies' mending room. Perhaps we might then discuss in private your progress in obtaining this letter." He tipped his hat. "That is, unless we are in the fortunate position of perusing it together."

* * *

Satisfied, Araminta stepped from the carriage. Sir Aubrey had been little short of rude to her when she'd hinted at being in a position to please him soon, so it would serve him right if she bestowed her favors upon Lord Debenham instead. And while Jane was not the only one to have relayed some disturbing stories about His Lordship, passed on to her by Jem, he was not only a viscount, but just two sickly cousins stood in the way of an earldom. Why, if she played her cards right and luck was on her side, she might one day become a duchess.

Still, Sir Aubrey was a great deal more personable. He was handsome and there was something roguishly appealing about his manner, but he was not as rich as Lord Debenham, which was sad. Nor, lately, had he been as responsive.

Really, she'd just have to wait and see how far the two gentlemen were prepared to reward her when all was said and done.

* * *

Hetty, alert to any sound that suggested Araminta's return, burst into their bedchamber shortly after she heard her sister's stealthy tread along the corridor.

"Where have you been?" she cried. "I've been nearly mad with worry. What did you think you were doing, going in my stead to see Jane's beau? Oh, don't look at me like that! I know very well what you've done and now you're coming downstairs with me to explain to Sir Aubrey."

Filled with relief and righteous anger, Hetty succeeded in dragging her sister into the drawing room which was, thankfully, empty of her parents, her mother still preparing herself for dinner and her father not having been seen since his morning walk.

Sir Aubrey rose when she entered and Hetty's heart clutched at the cool look on his face. Then Araminta swept into the center with the confidence of a queen and Hetty felt painful jealousy seep into her veins as her sister murmured, "Good afternoon, Sir Aubrey, what a surprise to see you here at such an unfashionable hour. I hope you won't object if I excuse myself shortly to dress." She sent him a regal smile. "I was late back from a walk with my Cousin Stephen and I fear my papa, who is a stickler for the proprieties, will be peevish if I do not present myself at the dinner table on time."

"You've been to see Jem and you've been gone hours!" Hetty cried.

Araminta sent her a maddeningly self-contained look of inquiry. "Jem?"

"You were on a clandestine mission." With difficulty Hetty reined in her ire. "I know everything and I know you saw what was written in that letter. Do you realize how dangerous this path is you've taken?"

Araminta leant against the back of the settee and examined her finely shaped fingernails. "I don't know what you're talking about, Hetty. Who is Jem and what letter is this you speak of?"

Sir Aubrey took a step forward and, to Hetty's outrage and despair, took Araminta's hand, turning her to look at him. "I believe damaging allegations were made in that letter which you know very well exists, Miss Partington." His tone was far too intimate for Hetty's liking. "Allegations questioning Lord Debenham's allegiance to his country, not to mention the writer's own feelings toward her husband. Perhaps you'd do me the great service of divulging what the letter contained."

Araminta smiled into his eyes. "Have no fear, Sir Aubrey, you were well spoken of by the writer, who felt only remorse. So sad," she added on a sigh, closing the gap an inch with no regard for Hetty. Or perhaps with only too much, for her sister enjoyed goading her and she was aware of Hetty's feelings for Sir Aubrey. "But nearly two years has passed since the writer—your wife—has been gone. It's time to move on."

"We really need to have possession of this letter, Miss Partington."

"Jem has it."

Angrily, Hetty said, "You've put Jem in danger, don't you know? Jane came to me not five minutes ago in great agitation, saying she'd had word from one of Lord Debenham's servants that

Jem has gone missing."

Araminta raised her eyebrows. "If we all got into a fluster when we were five minutes late, I don't know where we'd be."

Hetty stamped her foot. "You don't understand, Araminta. Lord Debenham didn't know for sure the letter existed until you told him. Now he'll go after Jem for it, for certain. That's if he hasn't already."

Araminta smiled. "Why would he do that? He gave me what was required to induce Jem to give me the letter. We have the matter all in hand. Really, I'm sure you're all much too concerned over Jem and, besides, the letter wasn't *too* bad though I can see why Lord Debenham wouldn't want the world to see it."

Boldly, Sir Aubrey put his arm about Araminta's shoulders and walked her to the window embrasure. Hetty could hear his voice, low and intimate as they stood talking. Dull misery churned in the pit of her stomach as she stared, straining to listen, into the fireplace.

"May I exhort you, Miss Partington, to try to recall the *exact* contents? You need to understand that what might not seem important to you could perhaps be very important." Sir Aubrey was speaking to Araminta as if she were a child and she, clearly, was enjoying the attention.

Hetty, slanting her gaze across at the pair, noticed that her sister's eyes sparkled as if this were the greatest of games. Or perhaps that was only for Hetty's benefit.

"Did the letter mention the name Spencean in relation to Lord Debenham?" asked Sir Aubrey.

A sly smile creased Araminta's brow. "Oh yes. I believe that's the club he belongs to." Her tone softened. "I know you want the letter made public so that it proves your wife regretted…certain decisions she made, but I'm sure the world won't judge you on that, Sir Aubrey."

"Araminta, don't you realize what you're saying?" Hetty cried, dashing forward to grip her sister's wrists, more to pull her away from Sir Aubrey than anything else. "If the letter calls Lord Debenham a Spencean and cites evidence, then of course Lord Debenham will do anything in his power to silence any who have seen or would speak of this letter. To be called a Spencean is to be called a traitor."

Araminta looked doubtful. "A traitor?"

"Traitors swing, Araminta!" Hetty heard the shrillness in her tone. "From the gallows."

She was glad this seemed to discompose Araminta.

Sir Aubrey's voice cut into the shocked silence. "A man who risks going to the gallows will do a great deal to ensure his secret is not divulged."

Hetty had to stop herself from stamping her foot when he again took her sister's hands and raised them to his lips.

"Did he ask you to meet him somewhere?"

It was clear that Debenham had by the way Araminta looked warily at him, though she refused to answer.

"I'd be very careful, Araminta. I mean it," Sir Aubrey said. "At the moment, Jem is missing. The butler is in high dudgeon and ready to boot him out of the front door when he deigns to show his face. I suspect that a young man who has gone to such pains to ensure he keeps his job would not risk being dismissed without a character lightly. I fear something has happened to him. For the moment, however, I want you to go over in your mind everything that was in that letter," gently he kissed each knuckle on her right hand, "and tell me."

Chapter Eleven

LORD PARTINGTON DID most of the talking at dinner that evening, which was unusual. He remarked upon the lackluster looks of his wife and the fact his usually dazzling Araminta was quieter than usual.

He didn't comment on Hetty. Probably because she was above notice, she reflected gloomily.

After dinner she went through to Araminta's bedchamber, where Jane was waiting to attend to her young ladies with tongs and sugar water. Jane looked drawn and her voice was shaky when she told them Jem was still missing.

Hetty noticed that not a flicker crossed Araminta's face. So her sister was going to pretend she hadn't been one of the last ones to have seen him.

Hetty plastered on a smile. "I'm sure there's some explanation," she reassured Jane though she felt far from hopeful, even with Sir Aubrey now in pursuit of the truth.

He had left them shortly after Araminta recalled what she could, though her sister had been vague about the contents and spoken only in generalities. Araminta had also sworn she'd made no arrangements to meet either Jem or Lord Debenham.

Hetty was alarmed, nevertheless. Araminta had spoken about Lady Margaret's shame and remorse over her disloyalty to her husband. And the letter seemed to link Lord Debenham with traitorous activities.

Even though Araminta could not remember in what context the word Spencean arose or how the sentence had been worded, her reconstruction painted Lord Debenham as a villain of the first order—even if Araminta still blithely maintained she was sure Spencean wasn't a word synonymous with traitor.

When Araminta left the room, Sir Aubrey had unexpectedly gripped Hetty's hands, pulling her to him in the window embrasure. Under the intense focus of his gaze, all the hopes and dreams Hetty had fostered regarding a future with this man were aroused.

But such hope was bittersweet and she knew she was only fooling herself, even when he'd said, "Keep a close eye on your sister. I will be at Lady Scott's tonight, where I look forward to partnering you in as many quadrilles and waltzes as are respectable." For an instant his promising words had thrilled her, accompanied as they were by the flash of promise in his eye. He'd then cupped her face, his expression more tender than she'd ever seen it. "Take care, little one," he'd whispered. "If I could only turn back the clock, I would."

Hope evaporated.

So he'd not find himself in such a compromising situation? she wondered dolefully.

Jane had finished dressing Hetty's hair and was busy with Araminta's when several taps upon the door had the young maid tossing the brush aside, saying, "Oh please, miss, I hope you're not cross but I was so out of me mind with fear I told Lizzie to give me a two-tap signal if something important were learned 'bout Jem's whereabouts."

Araminta nodded to her to leave the room and the sisters listened to the exchange of whispers in the passage before Jane burst in.

"They's found 'im in an alleyway with his head knocked in!" She began to cry. "Oh, lordy, it were my fault for telling 'is secret! He told me ill would come to him on account of me loose tongue and it has!"

Dismayed, Hetty asked, "Is he dead?"

"They thought 'e was 'til 'e stirred a little."

"Go to him, Jane," ordered Hetty.

Araminta was not so accommodating. "And what about my half a head of ringlets? It's hardly a look that will catch on."

Hetty couldn't care less what either of them looked like right then. Guilt clawed her insides but Jem's "accident" confirmed that finding the whereabouts of that letter was more important than ever. So, perhaps, was protecting Araminta, who had no idea of the danger she had caused others—and might be in herself.

Hetty glared at Araminta. "Take care how you conduct yourself tonight, Araminta," she warned as Jane fled into the passage. "You were the last to speak to Jem. I think it's hardly a coincidence that he is in such a way. Lord Debenham is behind this, mark my words."

* * *

Sir Aubrey's tender leave-taking was not followed up as Hetty had hoped, since the very first person he asked to dance was her sister.

Disgusted, she watched him lead Araminta into a waltz. The way the brazen thing responded was enough to make Hetty want the floor to swallow them up. First Araminta, then herself.

Over Araminta's shoulder she saw a familiar face beam its eagerness. Mr. Woking. Her heart plunged to the soles of her feet as his flabby lips stretched into an even more enormous smile as he hurried toward her.

Araminta and Sir Aubrey danced past her, their conversation making it clear how absorbed they were in one another. Picking up her skirts, Hetty hurried to the supper table to pretend an interest in the plover's eggs, glad to note Mr. Woking had been waylaid by an apparently garrulous dowager.

As she pierced a piece of ham upon her fork she gave a little sob, causing the young lady on her right to send her an odd look, which gained warmth as she said, "Why, we have met before, I believe." At Hetty's doubtful look, she added, "In the ladies' mending room though I cannot exactly recall which deadly dull entertainment it might have been."

Hetty restrained her surprise. The conversationalist barely resembled the tearstained young lady she remembered; although on second glance, her skin was still very bad and her figure not pretty. The glowing countenance, however, declared her a different person.

"Miss Hoskings! Of course I remember you!"

"That's right. The young lady who was about to make a disastrous match through self-doubt and ignorance." Miss Hoskings dun-colored ringlets bobbed while her beaming smile made her eyes twinkle like emeralds. Her pale green sarcenet did nothing for her coloring, its cut only amplifying her figure deficiencies but she carried herself with self confidence.

"So he has declared himself in the required gentlemanly manner?"

"Oh yes. Quite ardently in fact, and what pleasure it gave me to reject his kind offer." She giggled at Hetty's puzzlement. "Fortuitously I've come into an unexpected inheritance. The gentleman for whom I had misguidedly developed such a tendre approached me directly after my unexpected elevation to heiress to tell me I had quite the wrong end of the stick, if you don't mind my saying, and that he hadn't been intending to make an offer to anyone *but* me."

"So you'd prefer to keep your money and your single status?" Hetty wasn't sure she'd be able to if she were madly in love with someone. Well, she was madly in love with Sir Aubrey and now that she'd had time to think about it and regret her earlier reservations she didn't think if he asked her—outright—to marry him she'd be able to refuse under any circumstances, now. Even if she knew he wasn't in love with her. She'd just keep hoping like the foolish girl she was that she could change him. Make him love her.

"Well, I didn't reject him outright. I said if he could prove his love by waiting for me for a year while I study painting in Florence and take my favorite aunt on a grand tour across the Continent, I would probably reconsider my position."

Hetty attended to this with a frown while she rearranged the food on her plate. "Won't you...won't you miss him? That is, if you love him enough to want him for your husband."

The girlishness dropped away and Miss Hoskings gave Hetty a considered look. "I value my self-respect more," she said quietly. "And money has given me choices." Tossing back a ringlet, she became brisk. "Now you aren't looking at all the thing, Miss Partington. In fact, you look very much like I was feeling when we last met. If you need a comfortable bed to lie down on, there's a door behind that tapestry over there. It's hidden and no one knows about it but if you can't bring yourself to watch the one you love make eyes at another, I'd suggest you forget about food and take yourself off. The ladies' mending room is three rooms along the same corridor. Tell the chaperone that's where you're going but as there's no chaise longue there, I suggest you slip through the door hidden behind the tapestry and look for the second room along the passage to the right."

* * *

Sir Aubrey smiled into the exquisite face of the young woman in his arms and felt the tug of desire as she responded with a gentle squeeze of his hand. So subtle. So effective. She knew exactly how to play a man.

But she was not his sweet Henrietta.

Nevertheless, her endorsement of his interest evoked an unexpected plethora of emotions. Miss Araminta Partington would make the perfect wife. She was a beauty. Her father had a proud place among the top ten thousand and she came with a dowry that was not insubstantial. He foresaw important connections being made on account of having such a desirable wife when perhaps doors might have remained closed due to his tarnished reputation.

But, oh God, he wasn't in love with her, he was in love with her sister whom he'd be mad to marry, knowing how badly she desired it, and fearing how far short of her expectations he'd fall.

Right now, though, there were other matters of more importance.

Such as the letter that looked likely to clear his name and incriminate Debenham. If only the meddling minx in his arms had spoken to him first rather than trying to settle the matter, herself.

Aubrey managed a rather brittle smile in response to something she said, though he'd not been paying attention. He'd been preoccupied with the investigations he'd directed be made a little earlier, after the news regarding Debenham's valet's injuries. The lad had been found beaten to a pulp before being taken back to his room in the servants' attic at Lord Debenham's townhouse. It was the last place he should be!

Miss Partington slanted a knowing look at him, the candlelight reflecting the sheen of her glossy dark hair and making her eyes sparkle. "I trust you will be at the Grand Masquerade at Vauxhall tomorrow night, Sir Aubrey?"

"What person of consequence would miss the event of the season?"

She smiled coquettishly. "Who shall you fashion yourself after, sir?"

"Perhaps I would like to surprise you."

"I would like to be surprised by you."

The flirtatious banter was similar to many exchanges he'd enjoyed over the years with far less desirable women. The words dropped from his lips with ease and were received with veiled eagerness. He saw the flare of excitement in her eyes quickly shrouded by assumed world-weariness.

Was this what being a person of fashion required? The subsuming of real emotion? Again, dear Henrietta's unfettered enthusiasm sprang to mind. Her sheer delight at all the wondrous sensations to which he'd introduced her had been so unlike anything he'd experienced. She was perfectly delightful.

"Shall you appear grand and senatorial or wild and gladiatorial?"

He tilted his head and forced himself to smile back at her. He could do nothing about the letter until somehow he could speak to Debenham's valet, though that was not going to be easy.

So wasn't it better to court Miss Partington's goodwill since she offered a direct conduit, perhaps, to what he most wanted: vindication through the letter. She knew more than anyone else about what it contained and how to lay claim to it—unless Debenham had already laid claim to it. However, Aubrey suspected Debenham's thugs had been overenthusiastic in their dealings with the valet. There was a good chance the lad was too wounded to reveal his hiding place.

He clenched his jaw and told himself that dancing with Miss Partington was the pleasantest way to while away a few hours of an evening since his hands were tied when it came to following up on more serious matters.

The young lady was far and above the most beautiful in the room and he was conscious of the envious glances sent his way. A refreshing contrast to the covert suspicion he was used to, he thought, despite acknowledging it was his exquisite dancing partner who accounted for that. Not that Miss Partington looked so exquisite when she sized up her cousin's escort, a pretty young redhead in a modish coquelicot gown. Miss Partington clearly didn't like having competition, judging by her scowl.

But she would make a suitable wife.

It was, however, Stephen Cranbourne's disapproving glances that finally galvanized Aubrey into the realisation that with few options available to him, he must make some serious decisions, soon.

Either his name must be cleared or he must make a marriage that would see him received in all fashionable and political circles. An alliance of expediency with Miss Partington, particularly if she could indeed lay claim to the letter, would surely solve all his problems.

A marriage to Miss Henrietta underpinned with the hope of mutual love and desire was doomed to make them both unhappy before the ink was dry on the contract.

He lowered his head to whisper in her ear, "Wild and gladiatorial shall be the order of the day, Miss Partington." Drawing back, he smiled a knowing smile that equaled hers. "Be prepared."

* * *

Miserably, Hetty slipped through the doorway behind the tapestry. It had been easy to find though it was completely secret, shrouded as it was by a copy of the Bayeux Tapestry. When she neared the ladies' mending room, the chatter of excited debutantes threw her own mood into greater contrast. Never had she felt so wretched.

But before that was the room Miss Hoskings had mentioned, empty and dark save for the small fire in the grate and a lamp turned low upon the mantelpiece. How inviting the bed looked, she thought, as she sank upon it, closing her eyes. She'd like to lie here like Sleeping Beauty and not be disturbed for a hundred years. By then hopefully all her troubles would be over. Sir Aubrey would no longer exist though no doubt she'd be confronted with his many grandchildren, descendants of his marriage to Araminta. They'd be easy to spot with that streak of white hair contrasting with the dark.

The patent admiration upon Sir Aubrey's face as he'd gazed at her sister not ten minutes before still taunted her. As ever, Hetty was relegated to the sidelines, despite—or because—she'd given so much.

Well, wasn't that just typical of her? She'd never understood restraint; she'd always acted upon the impulses of her heart, in the here and now, with no thought to the consequences.

At least those consequences weren't of the direst. There would be no child and Sir Aubrey had chosen to accept the reprieve she'd given him in return for his silence. Her reputation was assured even if her virtue was no longer intact. She could consider herself in the same position as she was when she'd embarked upon her season with such mixed feelings—a hopeful wallflower.

A tear trickled down her cheek as she drifted into the sleep of dejected exhaustion. Just a few minutes to compose herself and then she'd return to the ballroom.

And so she slept, dreaming of handsome Sir Aubrey smiling down at her before Araminta pushed her aside and marched him down the aisle.

A loud exclamation brought her back to the present. She reared into a sitting position, blinking away the wooly-headedness as a voice muttered, "Good Lord, you're hardly the sister I expected! Don't tell me you're standing proxy for Miss Araminta?"

Hetty was really awake now, and nearly screamed in terror when she found herself the object of Lord Debenham's thunderous glare.

It swept across her skin in prickling waves as she cast a frantic look at the door. But they were alone and no help would be forthcoming.

"Gad, but I'd like to know what game you and your sister are playing at." Calculation had replaced his anger as he lent over her. In the flickering light his jet-black locks formed a devilish contrast with his alabaster skin. He pursed his thin lips. "As you may or may not be aware, I was expecting your sister, who declared every intention of being punctual for our little assignation. But you..." His expression soured. "Well, now that you're here, I'll simply state my case and leave you to ponder the consequences."

"Consequences?" Hetty managed to utter on a thread of sound. This man had a terrible secret to hide. He'd already proved himself capable of violence though thank the lord he did not seem to recognize her as Sir Aubrey's "plaything" as he'd termed it when he'd he tried to ravish her outside his townhouse when she'd been in masquerade.

She tried to look like the innocent debutante he ought to consider her. It certainly wasn't difficult to feign the necessary terror such a girl would feel in such circumstances. "I...can't imagine why my sister would agree to meet you, my lord." She swallowed. "Or what you want! Lady Scott directed me here when I told her I was feeling not quite up to par."

He was clearly in a less than charitable mood towards Araminta. What would he do to Hetty? He could hustle her out a back corridor and into the public arena, claiming she'd agreed to meet him...unless she acquiesced to some ghastly alternative. He would do that, she thought. Yes, he had the power to destroy her reputation unless she meekly acquiesced to whatever it was he wanted.

He put his head closer as he loomed over her, seeming to suck the very air from the room, from her lungs, and it was all she could do to remain sitting upright.

Acid dripped from his tone. "I trust you are anxious not to bring dishonor to your family."

Hetty could barely speak. "I don't know what you mean, sir. I…I was sleeping. I'd not expected to be disturbed. I need to be with my chaperone." *Dear Lord, surely Araminta hadn't dropped her in it. Surely she'd not told Lord Debenham of Hetty's involvement with the letter.*

He ignored her. "Don't play the innocent with me. Did you see my valet, or was it your sister? Ha! You're working together on this, aren't you? Blackmail, that's what it is, isn't it? Well, I could easily see every illusion Lord and Lady Partington have ever entertained about their precious daughter destroyed. Have you reduced to the dung heap of society."

The hatred in his eye seared her. No man had ever looked at her like this. With such feeling. Until she'd accidentally crossed Sir Aubrey's path, she'd never elicited anything other than vague, reluctant attention; attention that strayed in Araminta's direction the moment her sister flashed a calculated smile.

He hunkered down in front of her and gripped her shoulders. The touch of his cold fingers froze the blood in her veins. Now she had no choice but to scream but there was not enough air in her lungs.

"Pay attention, Miss Henrietta," he rasped, his hands straying to her neck. "If you do not bring me that letter, while remaining absolutely silent about it, I will ruin you and your family. You know where it is. My valet showed it to you at a coffee house yesterday, didn't he? Your sister told me that, and while she confidently claims she can restore it to me, I suspect that you are cleverer than she."

Hetty shook her head, wildly. "I can't possibly get it for you! Jem said he'd put it back in his hiding place."

"And where might that be? Jem's not in a position to tell me *anything* right now! You and your sister are the closest I have to claiming that wretched piece of parchment that is rightfully mine." His grip on her shoulders tightened and his voice became a low growl. "Your father is not too flush in the pocket right now, is he? Rumor has it he has made a poor investment decision. I, however, have the power to ameliorate his losses."

His breath warmed her cheek but his words chilled her heart.

"But only if you cooperate, Miss Henrietta," he whispered, and Hetty cried out in pain as he pinched her cheek. "Only if you fetch me the letter, which I know you will be able to do."

Trembling like a jelly, Hetty whispered, "Jem was set upon this evening and nearly killed. Y-you were behind that, weren't you?"

"Jem's demise was not my object." His mouth stretched, though not into a smile. "It was the letter I wanted but it was not on his person and he chose not to inform my henchmen of its whereabouts. Now you, Miss Henrietta, are in the ideal position to ensure that my wishes are carried out. Now that I think upon it, I believe it is far more fortuitous to find you here rather than your sister after all. Your maid is my valet's sweetheart. Yes, I discovered this today. I'm willing to let her to see her beloved on one condition: her sweetheart's future is assured *only* if she can persuade Jem to tell her where he's hidden that letter."

Hetty reared back as he stroked her cheek and a whimper rose in her throat as he touched her cheek. She forced it down. She'd not be reduced to a pathetic, puling child by his threats.

His expression softened in the dim light of the flickering candle upon the mantelpiece. His shadow, as he leaned forward, resembled a goblin's. "On the other hand, if you cooperate, I have the means to reduce your father's losses. All I need is that letter." With the tip of his finger he traced the line of her lips, his expression as rapt as if she were an object of great beauty. "You have the world at your fingertips, Miss Henrietta, for you have the power to make both your maid and my valet trust you when they would not me."

He rose from his haunches to his full height, his tone confident, ugly. "Now do not be so foolish as to do anything that forces my hand."

Hetty shook her head, for what alternative did she have? She felt like the terrified mouse she'd once seen before it was fed to the lion at the Tower of London.

Lord Debenham's shadow contorted terrifyingly upon the green and gold papered walls. "Good. I see at last you are being as sensible as your sister. Miss Araminta may not be as intelligent as you but she's canny enough to know that the damage to her reputation—and to her parents—would be irreparable were she to be caught alone in a room…with a chaise longue…and only me."

Hetty exhaled on a little sob. How could she ever have known the price she must pay for her sins would be such an impossible one? To lose her good name was one thing but to sacrifice her father and her family was intolerable. As intolerable as destroying Sir Aubrey's chances of regaining his reputation.

Lord Debenham chuckled. "No need to look so desperate." He sounded more cheerful now as he almost sauntered towards the door. "If you give me the letter, or can tell me where it is, it simply restores the status quo. Sir Aubrey will be no more maligned than he is now. Furthermore, your father's fortunes will be less damaged as a result of your good offices. Now, as to delivery, you have twenty-four hours to find that letter and to give it to me."

Hetty thought he was done with his threats but at the door he stopped and rubbed his chin. "Meet me at the third supper box on the walkway behind the orchestra at the Vauxhall Gardens Grand Masquerade tomorrow. *With the letter.* You will know me by my military attire. Alexander the Great, no less. I shall be there at ten o'clock, Miss Henrietta." He smiled. "And I do not expect to be as disappointed by your lack of punctuality as I have been by your sister's. Now go, Miss Henrietta! My nephew has been asking after you all evening and I do not want to suffer his disappointment if he does not get to stand up with you at least twice."

* * *

Araminta glanced up at Sir Aubrey and smiled. What a wonderful night it was. The orchestra was in fine form and she was in the arms of a handsome man. Yes, quite the most desirable man at the ball. Still, it would not be a bad thing to make her excuses and leave him wanting more.

She gave a despairing sigh. "I fear I must visit the ladies' mending room if I am not to put my foot through my trimming and make a public spectacle of myself, landing flat on my face as poor Hetty once did. You should have heard the company laugh."

"I would not have."

"Poor Hetty is such a plain little thing. She finds it very difficult that all the young men dismiss her in favor of," she tossed her head, "more desirable dance partners."

"I think her a charming companion."

Araminta sighed again. "You are so kind to spare her your attention. She's really so grateful."

"It's hardly a chore."

Araminta didn't like the way his mouth quirked. "She has her sights set on Mr. Woking, you know. It's the ideal match. Though not as handsome as some," she sent him a meaningful look, "he has a fine estate but much too remote for some ladies' tastes. Hetty is used to solitude. She will thrive."

"As the lonely wife of an ugly man?"

Araminta's mouth dropped open. Then realizing he was clearly sharing the joke with her, she tittered. "You really are too wicked, Sir Aubrey, the way you twist a girl's words."

"Just as long as I've reassured you as to who is the better man. You must not allow Lord Debenham to see that letter, my dear." The waltz had just come to an end and he drew her to the edge of the dance floor before taking her hands in his. Raising them to his lips, his expression was serious. "Lord Debenham is guilty of a heinous crime, Miss Partington. It's only a matter of time before justice catches up with him, either through the revelation of this letter or through other channels, and they do exist, my dear. His Lordship is on the path to ruin." Dropping her hands, he briefly caressed her cheek. "If you allied yourself to the right cause, I would be forever grateful."

Araminta smiled at him, murmuring as Hetty arrived in their midst, "In that case I promise to be worthy of such eternal warmth."

She knew Hetty's stricken look ought to make her feel bad but as she picked up her skirts and hurried through the ballroom, she consoled herself that it was kinder, all in all, that Hetty be disabused of any thoughts that Sir Aubrey reciprocated her feelings. He was certainly thoughtful and charitable toward her but more in the nature of a benevolent uncle toward an unprepossessing but sweet child.

Midnight had chimed some minutes ago and Lord Debenham would be waiting but Araminta knew that keeping an eager man in suspense only heightened the potential rewards.

Now, as she tiptoed in the direction of the ladies' mending room, careful to ensure she was unobserved as she sidled into the passage, she was conscious of her mixed emotions. Lord Debenham was frightening but somehow that only made him more exciting. Certainly she must manage this next interview with as much delicacy as she'd managed Jem. Satisfaction surged through her. She'd twisted Jem right around her little finger.

She'd have to be just as persuasive with Lord Debenham, though the final outcome depended on what he could offer her; for Sir Aubrey had been quite charming on the dance floor and he was clearly ready to make her an offer, too.

Now she just needed to make poor Jem—whom she was certain was going to make a complete recovery very soon—understand how important it was to give her the letter. Really, there was nothing that could not be bought at the right price.

She paused to smooth her hair and pinch her cheek while she contemplated on the wonderful choices at her fingertips. Lord Debenham or Sir Aubrey. Whom would she choose. When a young lady was as lovely and charming and persuasive as she, the world was her oyster and squandering large amounts of money to achieve her aims was not always necessary.

Chapter Twelve

"WHAT A CHARMING picture you girls make." Lady Partington looked at her daughters proudly as she entered Araminta's bedroom, where the girls were being dressed by Jane for the masquerade.

"And how are you, Jane?" she asked, her brow creased with concern as she put a hand on the girl's shoulder. "How is your Jem?"

Jane pretended great concentration in positioning a hairpin amongst the flowers of Hetty's headdress though the moistness of her eyes glistened in the firelight. "He's a little better today," she whispered. "Lord Debenham's own doctor is attending to him and I was allowed to visit 'im this mornin'."

Hetty was not surprised by Jane's lack of enthusiasm when her mother responded warmly, "How *kind* of Lord Debenham."

At the same time, revulsion tore through her at the mere mention of Lord Debenham's name, mingled with fear at what she'd set in motion. Jem had been injured because of her meddling. Araminta had made matters worse, but when all was said and done, Hetty was responsible.

She glanced across at her reticule that lay on her bed and her heart quailed at the thought of what she must do, for soon it would contain the letter which Jane had slipped her this morning.

She hated the thought but she would do as Lord Debenham had demanded in return for his promise that he would ensure Jem's safety and her father's fortunes.

Nothing would be any different from the way it was now, except that Jem, Hetty and her family would be safe and protected. Did she not owe them that?

Yet what of justice? Did Sir Aubrey not deserve to be publicly exonerated of the whispered charge of being a wife-beater and a Spencean?

A perusal of the letter after Jane had given it to her had

confirmed her worst fears. Lady Margaret had spoken candidly of Lord Debenham's involvement with those who'd attempted to assassinate Lord Castelreagh. She'd also written with the deepest remorse of her disloyalty toward her deserving husband.

She rolled her shoulders, uncomfortably aware of the stiff parchment that pricked her skin after she'd hastily tucked it down her décolletage and out of sight when she'd seen Araminta approach.

By rights the letter should go to Sir Aubrey but the dangers were too great. Who knew what villainy Lord Debenham was capable of? Hetty knew that the letter, on its own, would not be sufficient to shackle Lord Debenham - certainly not in the short term when he could do so much damage to them all.

No! The outcome that produced the least collective harm would be to give the letter to Lord Debenham, for then Jem, Jane and the entire Partington family would be safe and Sir Aubrey would continue as if nothing were any different. He'd managed thus far.

Lady Partington lowered her heavy bulk onto the bed. "Humphrey tells me that Lord Debenham has shown you particular interest, Araminta. It was mentioned at his club. Do you return his interest? I thought you had formed a tendre for Sir Aubrey though you know I have my reservations about him ..."

Her voice trailed off and Hetty glanced over at her, noting how large she looked. She seemed content these days, though she was clearly troubled now.

Araminta shrugged. "Cousin Stephen says Lord Debenham is set for an earldom and appears to be gaining favor at court which is all very good news because I really was in quite a dilemma, knowing that both he and Sir Aubrey looked set to make me an offer before the end of the week and I knew how much you disliked the idea of me marrying Sir Aubrey."

She glanced smugly at Hetty before returning to study her reflection, apparently consumed with the decision as to which pair of earrings best suited her costume as a Spanish dancing girl. "Now Mama," she added, deftly changing the subject, "you know Hetty wanted to go as a nun but wasn't I right in saying she should dress the same as me?"

Gloomily, Hetty looked down at her lavishly garbed form before sending her sister an envious glance. Araminta shone. Her glossy dark ringlets cascaded down her back, swallowed up by the crimson-and-black froth of her gown. By contrast Hetty felt a pale shadow of imitation. Her gown was identical and her hair, lighter and far less striking, also fell in ringlets but she did not have that elusive element her sister possessed to carry off the ensemble. The colors and the style simply did not suit her.

"Araminta insisted it would be amusing to be a pair," said Hetty, swallowing down the lump of emotion that threatened to turn into tears she'd have no idea how to explain.

"And you look lovely, darling," Lady Partington said, reaching for Hetty's hand when Araminta left the room to court their father's admiration. "Hetty dearest, Stephen tells me you have lost your heart to Sir Aubrey. Your cousin is very concerned. Please, my darling, listen to good advice and stay clear of a man whose reputation is under such a cloud."

It was an exercise in restraint not to break down as Hetty gazed into her mother's worried eyes. "Sir Aubrey is undeserving of society's low opinion." She heaved in a difficult breath to add, "Not that it matters, for he loves Araminta."

"Araminta will not ally herself with a man who cannot offer her the moon." Her mother sounded confident on this point. "Sir Aubrey is not a match for either of you. Don't look so sad. He is the first man to hold your interest but he won't be the last. You have the rest of the season before you."

"But no more after that, Mama. Has Papa said more about…his situation?"

Lady Partington dropped her gaze to the Aubusson carpet and sighed. "Developments are not what he had hoped…" Raising her head, she made an obvious effort to sound bolstering. "But that is nothing for you to worry about."

Hetty nodded, picking up her lavish skirts to move disconsolately toward the door. She was about to let herself out when impulse made her swing 'round to say urgently, "Mama, if you knew the truth about something or someone but it seemed better for all to withhold it, what would you do?"

Lady Partington looked startled. "My darling, without evidence, a truth is merely a rumor. Nothing can trump hard facts. Truth is always better revealed for the world to judge. Now, let me see a smile on that pretty face of yours. Your father remarked only a moment ago that you were turning into a swan. Just make sure you don't act impulsively when it comes to choosing a husband, Hetty. It would be wrong to take the first opportunity that comes your way simply because you think your father's situation dictates you must."

Jane waylaid her with a hand on her arm when she was in the passage. "Miss Hetty, yer sister's bin asking me for the letter I gave you. She flew into the boughs when I told her I didn't have it." The faith with which the little maid confided her next fears was like a dagger. "I couldn't bear the thought I'd given it to the wrong person, for I know she were intendin' to pass it straight on to Lord Debenham in return for his fancy promises. Yer can't believe that Lord Debenham, Jem says. And he reckons he can look after hisself and knows how to manage his lordship, so don't be worrying' about him, now."

To the wrong person.

Jane's words echoed 'round Hetty's head later as she sat in the family carriage squeezed between Cousin Amelia and Araminta on their way to the masquerade at Vauxhall.

So Araminta intended giving the letter to Lord Debenham? But what about the limpid looks she'd exchanged with Sir Aubrey? She didn't believe her sister's ingenuous claim to her mother that she'd discarded the idea of marrying Sir Aubrey. The way they'd looked at each other at the ball the previous night made her feel sick with despair.

She nodded her head at a question Cousin Amelia asked while her thoughts raced off on a different tangent. What was Araminta playing at? Fire, certainly, but was she pretending to Sir Aubrey that she was going to retrieve the letter from Jane to give to him when all the time she was intending to hand it to Lord Debenham?

With a self-pitying sniff, Hetty conceded that when all was said and done, she was the sister whose sins were the greater, on balance. She'd offered what no man could resist—a woman's body for the taking. Beyond the transitory physical trade there was nothing. She was nothing. And *now* where was the nobility in what she was going to do?

Nervously she felt, yet again, for the letter inside her reticule, where she'd transferred it, and was immediately swamped by nausea. Lord Debenham was dangerous. Violent. Unless he had the letter, her reputation was in ruins and consequently, so would her father's be and Jem would be without a job and perhaps in graver danger than he already was. Perhaps Araminta had intended to give Lord Debenham the letter in exchange for marriage—and who knew what else. She liked to live dangerously, after all.

Oh dear, but Hetty's mind was all over the place, imagining this and then that. But if Araminta were the one to give the letter to Lord Debenham, that would mean Sir Aubrey was free for Hetty. Perhaps Hetty should just hand it to Araminta. No! That, she could never do. Besides, Sir Aubrey would *never* marry Hetty. He could not have made that clearer.

Their country cousins were in their element. Squealing with delight at the lavish spectacle of so many fabulously garbed people, the two girls, dressed as shepherdesses, hurried their cassock-garbed brother into the melee, leaving Hetty to trail behind Araminta, who sashayed forth on Cousin Stephen's arm.

The crowd was thick and it wasn't until she was conscious of so many actually pressing in on her that Hetty realized Sir Aubrey was walking close beside her.

His smile made her insides turn to jelly but she stuck out her chin and pretended she didn't see him. The sudden spectacular explosion of fireworks caused a general shout of excitement and briefly Hetty found her hand encased in Sir Aubrey's large, comforting one.

Not knowing how it had happened and aware of her proximity to the rest of her family, she snatched it away as she tried to make herself immune to his charm.

She took a quavering breath as she stared straight ahead and her sense of justice perched heavily on her shoulders. The fact was, she could simply hand him the letter, here and now. Just slip it into his hand. Wouldn't it surprise him? She wouldn't expect anything in return but she'd know she'd done the right thing. Sir Aubrey was stronger and more powerful than Lord Debenham because he was good and he had right on his side. He would protect them all.

Yes, that's what she would do.

"I've missed you, Hetty."

Her mouth dropped open as she gripped her reticule tighter. He actually sounded sincere, but of course it must be an act. He'd gone to such pains to be charming to Araminta, too, and all because he wanted the letter and suspected either of them might have it, or be able to get it.

"I know I am not the one you're interested in," she said proudly, glancing across at Cousin Stephen to ensure he was not aware of their secret exchange, but unclasping her reticule nevertheless, for she could never give Lord Debenham what was rightfully Sir Aubrey's. She realised that now. "Araminta is over there."

She pointed. Her sister, in profile, looked utterly irresistible, her full lips parted in a smile of genuine delight, her eyes shining as she gazed about her.

"Her beauty is but skin deep. You are the engaging one," he murmured.

She stared back at him, trying not to allow her impulses to override good sense. Otherwise she might fling herself into his arms. Instead, she said in a rather brittle tone, "So you are trying to charm me into giving you the letter?" She was about to add that she was motivated by justice, not his honeyed words and then simply hand the letter over, when he spoiled everything by saying, "As a gambling man, my bets are that Miss Partington has it, given her greater powers of persuasion—no doubt backed up by threats." He arched an eyebrow. "Despite my attempts to charm Miss Araminta, I also suspect she has weighed up her options and has arrived at the conclusion that giving the letter to Lord Debenham will provide her with greater benefits."

Hetty swallowed down her indignation, her hand closing over the letter while she fumed inside. "Maybe you simply need to try harder to exert your charm upon her, Sir Aubrey."

The dark night sky was lit up with seemingly millions of stars as the fireworks exploded. The scent of gunpowder was strong but Sir Aubrey's own scent of sandalwood and leather was more thrilling.

His voice was now closer, warm with promise as it tickled Hetty's ear, charging her body with sensation which made her cross since he'd made it clear he did not love her enough to marry her. Self-consciously she patted the full net skirts of her ridiculously elaborate and furbelowed Spanish dancer's costume with her free hand, awaiting her moment. He might not love her enough to marry her but she'd still do the right thing.

"You're advising me to try harder to charm your sister? Nevertheless, you do not seem to relish that idea, Miss Henrietta."

She shrugged, forcing herself to sound distant. "I have no

thoughts on the matter either way."

An exploding Catherine Wheel sent a ripple of excitement through the crowd, pressing Hetty fully against Sir Aubrey's side. She felt lightheaded and completely thrown when he gripped her arm as if to steady her. Cousin Stephen and Araminta were a little ahead and had not yet noticed them.

"Are you angry that I've been making up to your sister?"

"It appears you need little encouragement to press your interest." Hetty twisted to glare at him. "The moment something more...enticing comes along, you show your true colors. I abhor inconstancy. However, despite that, I do have something that might interest—"

"Having experienced inconstancy with such painful results, I can assure you I feel the same way," he interrupted before his voice and manner changed completely and he lowered his head to say urgently, "Hetty, please forgive me for the distance I've allowed to keep us apart. You have every right to be hurt and angry—"

"Come, Hetty, let us listen to the orchestra." Araminta turned, a look of prurient interest sweeping across her face as she registered Sir Aubrey. Then Cousin Seb dragged her forward, pointing to the sky while Sir Aubrey whispered hastily in Hetty's ear, "I've secured a supper box. Druid's Walk. The same as last time. Hetty, I beg you, find a way to come to me."

Hetty tried to reach for him, call him back, but already he was moving away and then Araminta was on her right and Cousin Stephen on her left and Sir Aubrey was nowhere to be seen.

"Mozart or some refreshment?" Cousin Stephen quizzed the girls. "I suggest those who are for the former should take their seats here while the rest of us find something for our parched throats."

The three country cousins, plump and perspiring, were only too glad to slide into a seat while Hetty and Araminta elected to follow Stephen through the pressing crowd. They had only gone a couple yards before Araminta suddenly declared, "Cousin Stephen, I've changed my mind. I'll stay with the others."

Before he could reply, the crowd had swallowed her up. "Araminta!" Stephen called. "Wait!"

"I'll go with her," Hetty reassured him. "You continue, Cousin Stephen. I can see Mary and Amelia waving to us. Don't worry."

Already the jostling crowd was pushing him away from her as

Hetty, smaller and defter, was able to navigate her way through the melee.

Freedom, she thought with relief, only to find herself pinioned against a plaster bust by a large Corinthian, clearly in his cups, who barged past, causing her to drop her reticule. She had to wait for a straggling crowd to pass before she could look for it but Araminta had already got there first. Straightening, her sister held it out to her, her expression full of concern as she inquired if Hetty were hurt.

Hetty shook her head and Araminta hooked her arm in hers. "Hetty dearest, I'm so glad you followed me for I wanted to catch you alone," she said as they were steered by the crowd toward the orchestra pit. "I know you're upset that Sir Aubrey prefers me. He's been drawn to me from the first moment we met. I recognize that look in so many men's eyes."

They'd reached a quieter area now, a little away from the general hubbub.

"Has he made you an offer?" Hetty all but hissed, wondering if Sir Aubrey was planning to seduce Hetty later this evening before blithely announcing his betrothal to her sister. Surely he'd not do that? His sensibilities had been so upset when he discovered what he'd done to an innocent debutante, he'd barely touched Hetty since. Not until tonight, anyway, when just minutes ago he'd advertised his desire so clearly Hetty could not think he'd invite her to his supper box for any reason other than to...

Dare she believe it? Sir Aubrey was a man of honor. He'd never risk hers at this juncture unless it was to make her a respectable offer.

Araminta looked falsely sympathetic as only her sister could look. "Not yet but I expect one shortly."

Hetty glowered. "Only because he thinks you can get him the letter."

Araminta widened her eyes. "Oh no, just before we parted company last night I told him you had the letter," she said. "I wanted it but Jane declared she'd give it to you if she managed to get it from Jem and I know I won't induce you to hand it over to me." She sighed, adding, "Though as the eldest, I have every right simply to take it from you. But you're so eager to be the one to hand it over to Sir Aubrey." She gazed at the sky. "And if for some reason you didn't want to give it to him, Sir Aubrey said he'd find a way to persuade you." She swung 'round to smile at her sister again. "I decided to stay well clear of the nasty business but I did feel I owed you a forewarning of his intentions."

Hetty could barely see through her tear-filled eyes. "I'm sorry, Araminta, but I have to make an urgent visit and…and Seb and Amelia are waving to you. I won't get lost, I promise, but actually I rather think I'm going to be sick."

Dashing back into the throng before Araminta could respond, Hetty plunged along the Druid's Walk, making blindly for Sir Aubrey's supper box, Araminta's words screaming in her ears.

So his kindness was merely on account of wanting the letter? He was going to offer for Araminta tonight? Hetty was nothing but a credulous fool? He'd enjoyed toying with her but now he had no more use for her than a discarded…mistress?

"My love, what's the matter?" Sir Aubrey rose to his feet the moment she burst through the entrance and, completely against her earlier determination, Hetty allowed herself to be swept into his arms.

She fought the tears that stung her eyelids. She tried to be strong against his overtures but then his mouth covered hers in a deep and demanding kiss that sucked from her any resolve to hold herself aloof. How could she have believed Araminta? He *did* love Hetty.

The faint roughness of his cheek and his wonderful, familiar smell of all things manly overlaid with the strong soap he used reminded her so strongly of the happiest times of her life. He'd been truly drawn to her once so there was every reason he still was. He was a good man, she knew he was.

As she slithered, boneless, down the wall, he picked her up and carried her to the banquette, still kissing her with the passion of someone who has been starved of the physical and now seeks to plunder all that's on offer.

Helpless against her desire, Hetty kissed him back. She twined her hands behind his neck and pressed her body against his, glorying in the feel of his straining erection, a harbinger of the sensual delights she'd missed so much.

Until the terrible doubts and questions infiltrated her mind like fine mist, to counter the pleasure of his wandering hands.

Lying beneath him on the velvet cushioning she wrenched her face away from his. Of course she had to determine his motives before she allowed herself to make a fool of herself.

She could barely make out his features in the deep gloom for a single candle at the far end of the room provided the only light. His eyes, however, burned like coals in his face. "You're only doing this because you want the letter," she forced herself to say through trembling lips, staying his hand's progress at her knee. The skirts of her Spanish dancer's costume had been flipped up to reveal an expanse of bare thigh above her stocking. Quickly she pulled down the black lace froth to cover herself.

Sir Aubrey stilled as if she'd flung cold water at him. Only the sound of the fireworks, and their heavy breathing, punctuated the heavy silence. He looked angry. "Having the letter means nothing if I can't have you, my Henrietta," he said at last. Then he was smiling again, a faint sigh of desire gently vibrating against her lips as he ignored her protests, pushing away her hand to trail delicate fingertips the length of her thigh.

Hetty knew when she was defeated. His deft caresses, the tenderness and strength of his warm embrace and the wicked sensations Sir Aubrey had reawakened were almost too much.

Nevertheless she had enough strength to rasp through lips that stung with the need to press against his, "You want to seduce me so that I'll give you the letter and then you're going to marry Araminta, aren't you?"

This shocked him.

Dropping his hand abruptly from her leg, he set her away from him and sat up. He looked furious. "Good God, do you *truly* think me such a cad?"

Misery churned inside her as she watched him lounging against the pillows. He was frowning but he had not refuted it. Sir Aubrey was charming. He'd find a way to win her over, she knew it. She was weak when he was near and he was the only man she'd ever wanted. Would it make her feel better to hear him admit the truth, or deny it? At least then she could fool herself after she allowed him to make love to her one last time, her excuse being that she'd believed he was going to make an honorable woman of her.

She sucked in a difficult breath as she met his troubled gaze. "How could I think such a thing? Why, the look that creeps into your eye every time you speak to Araminta tells me so. That, coupled with the ease with which you know you can have me." She looked away, the miserable truth weighing her down. "I knew it was madness for me to come here. I knew I would be completely won over by your charm and that I was a fool for being so weak. You could just take what was on offer. There was no chase for you. I have only myself to blame when you discard me."

"Hetty, no!" He shook her gently, real anger in his eyes. "Is that what you think? That my only interest is in what you can offer me? Your body? The letter?"

Then he was kissing her again and she was across his lap, supported by his left arm while being pleasured with his right, his fingers blazing a trail of sensation up her thigh, and she had no more willpower than a butterfly in a field of buttercups.

"I want you, Hetty, more than I want that damned letter," he growled. "Araminta holds no interest for me, even if she does possess it."

"You can't be serious." The words came out as a croak for his fingers continued their magical caresses and her mind was fast becoming swamped by the lustful sensations created. She would not question her actions later but she knew already she would succumb. He was everything she'd ever wanted.

"Deadly serious." He stopped kissing her, the expression in his eye warning her to take heed. "Araminta is cold, mercurial…calculating. Perhaps I shouldn't condemn her for that since every woman needs to position herself as well as she can in this world. But you, Hetty…" His expression softened. "You are quite unlike anyone I've ever met. You're warm and soft and…completely disarming with your ability to give."

Hetty gave a self-deprecating laugh, not convinced in this regard though his kindness and the purely physical sensations he continued to evoke in her were close to mind-altering. "Like I'm giving myself to you now?"

The faintest of shrugs and a return to pleasuring her were his answers and Hetty whimpered as she fell back into his arms, her body thrilling to the heightened sensation.

"Your willingness and your genuine pleasure in my attentions endorse your sincerity and bolster my reasons for begging you to meet me."

She stiffened. "To seduce me?"

"To make you my wife."

She gave herself a little shake and opened her eyes once more, the warmth of his smile reassuring her that she'd heard correctly.

"My wife, Hetty," he repeated, though she'd said nothing. The darkening of his eyes and the tensing around his mouth bore out his next words as he straightened and put his hands on her shoulders. "The last few days have been torment. I've thought my fevered agitation was due to the letter being so within my reach. Then I realized I'd lived without it so long that it barely mattered any more. Time was erasing the slur upon my good name and it wasn't in fact the letter I longed to get my hands on…it was you."

She stared. Then through constricted airways she breathed, "You're asking me to marry you?"

He nodded, bringing his face close to hers. "I'll do it properly, on bended knee in a moment, but yes, I'm asking you to marry me."

The pressure inside her was nearly unbearable. She longed to feel his body respond with hers. Not just now, but forever. Yet she had to ask the question. "Why?"

"Because I love you," he said simply. "I have never loved anyone like I love you." He rolled his eyes then flipped up her skirts and skimmed her thighs with the flat of his hand before patting them down respectably. "And because I find your luscious curves even more desirable than the first time I became acquainted with them during our unexpected introduction." Before Hetty could respond, he drew down the lace at her décolletage and bent his head to kiss the nipple he'd deftly exposed, circling it with his tongue before gently sucking on it, making Hetty writhe and whimper. Raising his head, he muttered wickedly, "And I know you are the only woman I'll enjoy talking to with the same enthusiasm I shall devote to our lovemaking."

His hot, moist breath was driving her mad with lust. She wanted him as much as she wanted to hear his words. Wanted to be clasped within his naked embrace so they both could share this moment equally.

But he seemed happy to take his time. Or rather, murmur in the most deliciously intimate way while he sent her to Heaven and back.

Hetty was registering on two levels. While her body was pulsing with need, her heart was growing fuller by the moment, the more he explained the effect she had on him, first in physical terms, before he then patted her clothing respectably back into place.

"But then I became acquainted with your sweet nature..." Moving his face up, he kissed her brow, her eyes and nose and then finally her lips as he finished, "And your wonderful capacity for love and forgiveness. You are the complete woman, Hetty." He cupped her face with his hands and gazed at her as if she truly were an angel. "Your body, mind and sweet nature are without equal. And I've realized I don't want to settle for less. Will you accept my offer, Hetty? Will you be my wife?"

What a question? He'd well and truly convinced her of his sincerity and her joy knew no bounds.

"Oh yes," she whispered, her hand straying to the flap of his breeches. "Oh yes, Sir Aubrey, and now you must take your pleasure too."

She registered the amusement in his voice as he asked, "What makes you think I'm not enjoying your responses enough to satisfy me? We are not yet wed, Hetty, and I am mindful of your reputation. Whatever the temptations, I set out tonight determined to draw from you the response I wanted and to resist the temptation of taking advantage of you until we are legally bound together as husband and wife."

"But that'll be weeks!" she cried, her dismay making him laugh and draw her back to him, tightening his hold on her.

Trailing kisses along her jawline, he said softly, "I'm glad to hear you are as impatient as I. But dearest Hetty, I am an honorable man and an honorable man does not intentionally deflower a virgin. Hush!" He laid a finger gently over her lips to stop her protest.

"You gave me a way out and I'd have taken it, had I truly not wished to marry you. I told myself you would be better off given your freedom but within a day I was tormented by thoughts of what I was throwing away." He kissed her again, his voice warm with love as he held her to him once again. "I love you, Hetty. I want to look after you, cherish you and make you happy. I want you to love me and have my children but I'm an honorable man and I will not risk your good name until we are legally wed. Today I have gained your father's consent—yes, even despite the slur to my reputation." He laughed and to her surprise he sounded genuinely happy. "I happen to count the Archbishop of Canterbury amongst my friends and so have organized a special license. His representative will be arriving here in half an hour to marry us."

"In a supper box in Vauxhall Gardens?"

The soft, gentle pressure of his hand stroking her cheek made her close her eyes briefly as she floated on her happiness. Surreptitiously, she ran her own hands the length of him but he gently captured them in his own.

"Patience, Hetty," he murmured. "In an hour, when you are my wife, we can both partake without fear and without guilt. But for now, your virtue remains safe with me."

She felt light and joyful as he helped her to her feet. He loved her. He'd said it in so many words and now he was going to prove it.

Cupping her face, he stared into her eyes. "I want to hear you say something, Hetty. Something that makes me believe you want this as much as I do…because you *love* me, not because you need to make a good match by the end of the season."

She took a deep breath and smiled, her mouth stretching into a wide, irrepressible grin. The joy that she'd expected to subside only grew more intense. She swayed with it until he steadied her with a smile that matched hers.

"Oh yes, Sir Aubrey, I'll marry you!" Breathlessly, she reached for her reticule, which had fallen to the floor. "And if in the past there were those who'd have said I was marrying a dangerous gentlemen, I now have the evidence that will make them eat their words." In just seconds she could prove her love beyond doubt. She fumbled for the letter within the delicately embroidered bag as she straightened, her excitement growing as she saw first his questioning look then the anticipation on his face. "However, once *this* is made public there will be no more false rumors." Her seeking fingers explored the silk interior of her bag and her stomach churned with impatience as the letter continued to elude her.

Her handkerchief made a soft wad of cloth in the bottom but there was no sharp edge of parchment.

Where was it? Where was the letter she'd transferred from beneath her chemise earlier that evening?

An image flashed through her mind of Araminta handing back her reticule after Hetty had dropped it amidst the stampede. Desperately she continued to rummage for the letter but it was not there. *Araminta?* Could she *really* have done this to her? With a despairing cry, Hetty tossed away the reticule as she sank against the wall, covering her face with her hands. She felt hollow inside. Hollow and small; bested once again by her poisonous sister. "Sir

Aubrey, I had the letter!" she wailed, nearly choking on the bitterness of having victory snatched from her hands in such a way. "Truly I did and now it's gone."

Blinking open her eyes she wasn't sure if doubt or disappointment clouded his expression, though it was difficult to make out anything in the dim room. He loomed over her but she shook her head, choking on another sob. "I came here with the express purpose of delivering it to you." She might have dissolved into tears except that suddenly disappointment turned to icy resolve. "And I *shall*," she vowed, as she swung toward the door, avoiding his outstretched hand. Grimly she added over her shoulder, "I know exactly where that letter is and I shall have it with me when I return."

Sir Aubrey gripped her wrist and pulled her back to him. "My offer is not dependent on that letter." His voice was urgent. "Don't leave. I know you are pure of heart, Hetty. I know you'd do anything to help me... And you have." His expression softened as he brought his face close to hers. "You have made me realize life's true priorities. That love and honesty are more important than advancement and material gain. Happiness is based on neither of those but rather the mutual felicity and affection between two worthy people. I want you, Hetty. I want you to be my wife and to enjoy you forever."

Footsteps crunching on the walkway made them draw away guiltily, a short rap on the door seeming to underline their recent transgressions. However, when a solemn-faced clergyman was shown in, Hetty gasped with delighted surprise, squeezing shut her eyes at the sheer joy of her suddenly altered situation, her disappointment at the loss of the letter for the moment forgotten.

When she opened them it was to the thought that never in her wildest imaginings could she believe her dreams would come true. She truly was going to marry the man who had captured her heart. He'd declared in the most sincere and ardent of terms his love and desire and now, here was the clergyman he'd summoned.

Reality seemed suspended as the reverend performed the rites, Hetty murmuring her responses, Sir Aubrey speaking with firm conviction as he slipped the ring upon her finger, his eyes kindling with warmth, his smile reassuring her that this was everything he wanted.

"I'm sure you never imagined you'd dress as a Spanish

dancing girl for your wedding," he teased at the conclusion of the unexpected ceremony and once the clergyman had departed.

"I never imagined I would marry at all," she admitted, sinking against him and closing her eyes in rapture. "Araminta is the beauty. She's a bird of paradise and I'm a little brown peahen. Papa used to say it all the time."

"And you decided you were destined to live up to this description?" Sir Aubrey tipped her head up with a gentle finger beneath her chin. His mouth pursed with amusement. "Until you were so afraid for your life you thought giving yourself to me was the only way to preserve it."

He started to pull her closer but Hetty stayed him with a hand upon his chest.

"Now it is my turn to redress the balance."

She had the means and she should have acted earlier, before Araminta could pass on the letter to Lord Debenham. Hetty was married now and Araminta no longer posed a threat to her happiness. But Hetty could secure even greater happiness for her new husband if she hurried. Sir Aubrey, from his position of greater power, in consequence of her actions, would ensure Lord Debenham was a spent force and unable to harm her family or Jem.

"I promised I would restore the letter...where it would do least harm and achieve the greatest good," she told him. Her new husband must never know that she'd entertained, even for a short while, the intention of giving it to Lord Debenham.

But if she didn't hurry, that's just who would be receiving it.

"Hetty! Where are you going? Won't you stay—" He pulled her back to him, his lip curling with suppressed amusement despite her sudden urgency to get away. "For the finale? Now that it's legal?"

"Oh, my darling, I promise you the greatest finale," she replied, reaching up to kiss him quickly on the lips. "You stay right here, make yourself very comfortable and be prepared for my triumphant return." Running her hands down his thighs, she whispered, "I have a surprise for you, my love, and I do recall hearing you say once that all good things were worth waiting for."

Chapter Thirteen

ARAMINTA EYED HER prattling cousin with a decided lack of felicity as she sat wedged between the two young women who were ogling all the passing gentlemen with absolutely no shame.

She was embarrassed to be with girls who reeked of country and lacked address. Worse was wondering where Hetty was. Her sister had dashed off into the shrubbery, claiming nature called and reassuring her she'd return shortly.

But she hadn't and there was not a thing Araminta could do. Oh, she knew Lord Debenham was waiting for her in the third supper box behind the orchestra but he'd be waiting for a long time. He was not going to get the letter Araminta had snatched after Hetty had fortuitously dropped her reticule.

It was tedious having to bear her cousins' company while she listened to the strains of Mozart drifting into the starry night air but she relieved the boredom by contemplating Hetty's dismay at discovering her trophy gone.

No doubt Hetty planned to hand it to Sir Aubrey.

Despite reassuring herself that Sir Aubrey would rather wed an orangutan than her sister, Araminta simply could not rid herself of that shocking single glance she'd intercepted when Sir Aubrey had looked at her sister. She'd almost describe it as mawkish except that Sir Aubrey was certainly not mawkish.

Hetty was the ugly duckling of the family and it would be kinder to keep her hopes in check.

When she saw her sister hurrying toward them from the Druid's Walk, she leapt up, making her excuses to her cousins in order to waylay Hetty near the fountain.

Hetty stopped short when she was several feet away, startling Araminta with her hostility.

"What have you done with Sir Aubrey's letter? You took it from my reticule. I know it was you!"

When Araminta tried to calm her with a conciliatory hand

upon her shoulder, Hetty threw it off, muttering, "You've given it to Lord Debenham, haven't you? You're a fiend."

Poor Hetty, thought Araminta. Clearly she'd returned disappointed from her assignation to hand over the letter to Sir Aubrey who, if she wasn't mistaken, had hired one of the supper boxes in the darkened walkway from which Hetty had just emerged.

She tried to be placating. "Dearest, if you're so upset, perhaps you might try to persuade Lord Debenham to give it to you. I can tell you exactly where to find him."

She was amused when her sister actually stamped her foot.

"You can take me to him and demand the letter back because you had no right to give it to him in the first place."

"I'll do no such thing, however if you're brave enough to confront Sir Aubrey, you're brave enough to find Lord Debenham." She gave Hetty another condescending pat on the shoulder. "I promise I won't tell."

"Hetty, come and sit with us! Where have you been?" Their cousins had them in their sights and were signaling, clustered around a large bust of Caesar atop a plaster plinth. Araminta thought they looked like they'd just stepped off the coach from some remote region of the country where the locals wore turnips and carrots in their hats, for that's exactly what the trimming of the hideous confection Cousin Amelia wore on her head reminded her of.

Hetty turned on her heel with a disgusted look at Araminta, her breath coming in gulping sobs.

"My goodness but you are upset, my dear," Araminta soothed. "Perhaps it's not such a good idea, facing Lord Debenham in such a state. And of course you cannot do so unchaperoned. In fact, I can't imagine what possessed me to suggest something so ruinous." Araminta felt a stab of doubt. Hetty looked mutinous and if word got back to Mama and Papa that Araminta had induced her to seek out a gentleman alone, it was beyond saying there would be worse than the devil to pay. It would signal the end of Hetty's matrimonial hopes. Not that her sister had any realistic ones, it was true.

In a quick reversal, Araminta reconsidered. She must do whatever necessary to occupy Hetty for the next few minutes. Araminta was about to make her own sacrifice to save the family and she couldn't risk Hetty threatening a glorious outcome. Calling to her cousins that she would accompany her sister since 'nature called' right at that moment, Araminta took Hetty's arm and led her toward the darkened lane behind the orchestra.

"He is waiting in the third supper box," she murmured, pointing. "Here, sit down a moment to cool your anger. It is best you don't let it get the better of you, though. There is your reputation to consider and we are both courting disaster as it is. The cousins are just a short walk away and Cousin Stephen is too involved in the music to even notice us, so you just decide what you want to do." She hesitated. "I'm sorry about the letter but I did what I thought best."

She really was about to do what was best. Best for the entire family, Araminta thought some minutes later as she sauntered briskly along the dimly lit path from which her sister had emerged. This was a mission no lady ought to embark upon but she was confident of her ultimate success.

It was the only way they'd all find happiness. It would be the answer to her father's problems. Sir Aubrey's good name would soon be cleared and in consequence he'd be even richer.

She couldn't think of a better catch than Sir Aubrey, for the idea of being allied to Lord Debenham was again losing its luster. He had a cold menace about him. Initially it had intrigued her when she'd felt certain of twisting him 'round her little finger. Now she was uncertain of her power to enslave him, which meant marriage to him would not be worth the compensations provided by multiple estates and fine clothes. He was too much a wild card. Even Araminta, so confident of her charms, was not entirely confident she could hold him sufficiently in thrall.

Sir Aubrey was a different matter altogether. He was deeply honorable. The kind of man who would never dishonor a woman without proper atonement. The trouble was, she wasn't as confident of his affections as she'd like to be. Certainly, he'd made up to her in a very pretty fashion during the past few entertainments. The roiling passion in the depths of his eyes had thrilled her but the more she reflected on the way he looked at her little sister, the more unsettled she became.

Well, now she had the letter. All she need do was present it to him and he'd be hers. She might have to work for her reward but that would hardly be a chore.

The sight of his distinctive silver-topped cane by the door to the supper box was confirmation that her mission was on the way toward being successful.

Approaching stealthily, she was surprised at the roar of blood to her head and the rapid beating of her heart. She was not used to such sensations and she liked them. She felt exhilarated and alive.

The dismaying thought intruded that perhaps he wasn't alone. Her fears were soon put to rest. When she carefully opened the door a lazy, laconic voice drifted through the darkness.

"Come to me, my darling."

Araminta nearly fainted on the spot. He was expecting her?

Then another, even more shocking thought ripped through her. He was expecting someone else?

Hetty?

No, it was not possible. A woman of the night?

It didn't make sense. Sir Aubrey would never have planned an assignation with her unprepossessing and far less worthy sister.

The possibility that he had was enough to galvanize the most gently reared beauty into action. Sir Aubrey was not going to offer for Hetty, leaving Araminta, the beautiful, worthy eldest sister, to cool her heels for another season. No, he would not.

And when Araminta's work was done with him there would be no way he could! Her heart rate rapidly accelerated and her breathing rasped in her throat. She had to carry this off, knowing the hopes of the entire Partington family rested on her success?

Faint strains of Mozart hung in the air. The room was in almost complete darkness, lit only by the light from the hanging lamp outside the door.

Quietly she entered, and it seemed like divine inspiration to snatch an end of the gauze drapery that divided the room in two and drape it over her head and the full net skirts of her costume, to further disguise her natural shape.

"Hetty? Is that you, my darling? Come to me. My, my, so *this* is what you had in store for me."

Araminta froze, not believing what she was hearing, for amusement and anticipation colored his tone as he started to rise, though Araminta was quick to indicate he should remain where he was. She had a show to put on.

Her outrage hardened when he seemed to think it a splendid idea—as if her sister were capable of the kind of entertainment Araminta was about to perform.

Slowly she swayed to the strains of music that drifted in from the night but then, realizing Sir Aubrey might be not quite as delighted as she'd hitherto expected to discover her real identity, Araminta decided to cut short her overtures. Much more important than courting his admiration was swift action on her behalf to make sure he was in her power. She pulled her thick lace mantilla more thoroughly over her face and, taking a deep breath as she leant over him, boldly ran her hands up his thighs before stepping back quickly.

"Good Lord, but you are full of surprises." His voice was a low, needy growl that sent anger pulsing through Araminta. How dare he speak like that, believing she was plain, dull Hetty? The glazed rapture of his expression only added to Araminta's determination to continue this…clinical seduction, as it now appeared it would have to be.

To the bitter end, in fact.

"Ah, so you want me to close my eyes while you do all the work for a change? All right, then, I am your slave. And hark, we have the fireworks outside to celebrate."

Dear God, what did that mean? If Sir Aubrey really did believe she was Hetty, then she was succeeding in whipping up his desire much too quickly, Araminta thought, as she took in the ecstasy that sharpened his expression, though they were in almost total darkness. Right now she might appear a mysterious figure full of allure and promise but once she was done with him, he'd realize which sister offered him the future he wanted.

His breathing was labored and the effect of her calculated progress as he lay back upon the cushions was clear. His tight satin breeches bulged with his enormous erection. Had Araminta not been so fueled by spite and anger, she'd be anticipating this as much as he clearly was. Yet he thought she was Hetty…

All her delicate sensibilities recoiled at the travesty.

"Oh, my darling, you are torturing me. Come to me now."

Shocked, Araminta saw that his hand had gone to the button flap of his breeches. How could he imagine Hetty would ever—?

Good Lord, she'd never have believed such a thing possible if it weren't happening before her eyes. Her sister? Plump, undesirable Hetty, who was surely beneath Sir Aubrey's notice? Rapidly she cast her mind back over the past couple of weeks but could put her finger on nothing of note. Yet every indication now pointed to

Hetty having been very free and easy with her affections, while keeping a decidedly low profile. Araminta, on the other hand, would never be so bold without the promise of a ring.

Or at least the knowledge that her actions would secure her a ring very shortly.

But desperate times called for desperate measures. This was the only way forward. Her father was clearly about to ruin them all and if Araminta did not contract a good marriage by the end of the season, there was a real chance she was not going to at all.

If Sir Aubrey was going to marry, then it was going to be a Partington—and certainly not the younger one!

With another tug to ensure the mantilla gave her the anonymity she needed, Araminta trailed one hand over her breasts in an overt display of self-admiration before gripping the hem of her skirt and raising it above her knees.

"My God, woman, but you are a minx," growled Sir Aubrey who had clearly opened at least one eye. "Come here now!"

His arms were outstretched and the strain in his voice indicated his impatience. Araminta nearly wept at the injustice but it was the impetus she needed. Launching forward as she breached the separation of the gauze curtain, she landed upon his chest, hitching up her skirts to find him already released from his breeches.

Her breath left her in a cry more of satisfaction than rapture as she impaled herself upon his pulsing member.

She was hungry for him—or rather, hungry for vengeance— her passage well lubricated by the anticipation she'd whipped up. Clearly Lord Aubrey had also reached the pinnacle of his desire, for no sooner had she plunged herself upon him and begun to writhe in ecstasy than he gave a harsh cry.

Her satisfaction was short-lived. In fact, it did not go beyond the moan he'd uttered as he convulsed inside her. For almost immediately he withdrew and, with a shout she'd almost say was anger, shoved her off his lap and leapt to his feet.

He was now staring down at her as if she were...well, certainly not a woman he desired.

Araminta was not prepared for this. She'd expected him to be surprised, but she'd not expected to see his lip twitching with the same disgust mirrored in his cold stare.

"For the love of God, woman, what have you done?" he

rasped, fumbling to button his breeches. "I thought you were—"

Anger bubbled up inside Araminta as she pushed down her skirts and sat up from her undignified position on the floor. "You thought I was…?"

Ignoring her as he strode towards the door, he swung around to demand, "Miss Partington, what the devil possessed you? Surely you can't have known—"

He was unable to complete a sentence, so great was his agitation.

"You seemed to enjoy it," she muttered, rising to her feet. "You didn't stop. You do realize it's more than possible I'm carrying your child, Sir Aubrey."

Not that she'd had much pleasure from it. A great ache of need still pulsed between her legs but that was nothing compared to the humiliation of being rejected. He should be reaching for her by now. Begging for her forgiveness and promising a wedding ring for having taken her virtue. Well, for seducing her, at any rate. Pushing out her chin as she gripped an upright beam, she said proudly, "It's what you indicated you were after, Sir Aubrey, let's not tiptoe around the truth. Those stolen kisses in the passage behind the tapestry. And not just at Lady Knox's ball."

His face was black with anger as he bent and gripped her shoulders, his teeth bared, like some terrifying wild animal. She nearly drew back but she had to remind him what he owed her.

"I had no idea it was you, Miss Partington, nor was I in a position to stop after you hurled yourself upon me and…no, I did not indicate that was what I was after!"

She must not cry. Pride and righteous indignation must be the order of the day. Nevertheless, her voice shook. "Yes, you did. Again, last night at the ball, you made your…desire…quite clear."

"A gentleman doesn't expect to be accosted by a lady in such a manner, no matter how much interest he shows her." His pupils were dilated, the words rasping from his throat, and he was looking at her as if she were some…hideous great spider.

"I gave you what you made quite clear you wanted, Sir Aubrey," she hissed. "I make no apology for that. You're the one in the wrong for giving me false ideas if in fact that *wasn't* what you wanted. But the deed is done."

Realizing by the lack of felicity in his expression that she was going too far, she adopted another approach. Forcing down her fury, she said in a quiet, controlled tone, "I'm upset, sir, that you take this attitude. I...I was hoping to give you a very pleasant surprise."

"A surprise indeed!" he muttered, drawing his hand across his brow as if he were unutterably weary rather than exulted at having taken the virtue of London's most desirable debutante. "Where is your sister?"

That was the last question she needed to hear when she'd been imagining something more along the lines of "Miss Araminta, will you consent to be my..."

Squaring her shoulders, she said, haughtily, "Gone to give Lord Debenham a certain letter, Sir Aubrey."

His sudden stillness was heartening, as was his chilly tone. "What did you say?"

Araminta tossed her head. "I told you. She is visiting Lord Debenham at this very moment to give him your letter."

"I don't believe you." Pointing to the now open door, he muttered, "Take me to your sister," before propelling her none too gently before him, closing the door behind them, upon all Araminta's high hopes.

* * *

The moment Hetty found herself face-to-face with Lord Debenham, she realized she'd made a grave miscalculation. For a start, she was alone and defenseless.

And he was clearly in a dangerous mood. What had she been thinking?

She hadn't been thinking at all. She'd been forced by desperation into finding the one thing she knew Sir Aubrey—she gulped, her new husband—deserved above all else.

In part Araminta's taunts had motivated her to show her sister that she would prevail.

"You are asking me for the letter? Ha! That's rich!"

How louche he looked, the smell of arrack upon his breath, the empty bottle lying in a corner.

Unfortunately Hetty had arrived in such haste, with heaving chest and eyes blazing, she'd noticed too late his disreputable state. He'd merely raised his glass to her in a mock toast before tossing back the liquor, his own eyes scorching as they'd raked her from head to toe.

"Without your sister beside you, you're not too hard to look at, little one. Come closer," he'd said.

But when Hetty had responded acidly that she'd rather approach a cobra, he'd turned nasty.

Now through narrowed eyes he replied, "I think your sister is the only person who can tell you where that letter is." He got to his feet, his expression filled with such menace that for a moment Hetty thought she'd faint clean away.

Instead, she calculated the distance between her back and the door but he was too quick. Seizing her wrist, he jerked her toward him and, gripping her chin, brought his face close to hers. So close she thought he was going to…bite her. For there was no tenderness in his expression as he said between lips pulled tight, "How might we induce that sister of yours to hand over what she clearly intends to profit by? You, my little one? Her baby sister? Do you think my threats against her precious sister will be sufficient?" He gave a short laugh, his eyes boring into hers, his lip curled in a sneer. "No, I didn't think so either."

She squirmed in disgust at the swell of his erection against her belly, recoiling from his breath moist against her ear as he ran his hands all over her. Terror bubbled up inside her but she was unable to force it out in a scream. It was as if every life-preserving instinct had been paralyzed.

"Perhaps the good name of the family is something she'd value more."

"Please don't!" Hetty whimpered, twisting in his cruel embrace as he buried his face between her breasts and his hands roamed freely.

"The disappointment is that you're already spoiled goods, aren't you?" He glared at her while she struggled ineffectually. "Yes, I've guessed your little secret. If Sir Aubrey hadn't already defiled you, he might be called upon to object." His ragged breaths were coming faster now as his grasping fingers pinched her nipples painfully and his mouth latched on to her ear.

Strength surged through her. "Get away from me!" she shrieked, louder now, hearing the tear of fabric and trying not to cry. She looked down at her ruined bodice and tried to pull her skirts down but he'd pinioned her against the wall and his seeking hands were too strong for her to push away.

"You're more adventurous than I gave you credit for, Miss Henrietta. Comelier and more desirable now I have you up close." He licked his lips as he gripped her thighs. "I think you must be a fiery morsel in bed else Sir Aubrey would not have spared you the attention he did. Oh, it's hard to credit but suddenly I understand everything."

"I'll see that you're brought to justice," squealed Hetty, terror making her shrill. "That letter could have you swing! Unless you want that, you'd better let me go."

"You really think such a threat is likely to make me release you?" He looked disbelieving. "The fewer witnesses to what is written in that letter, the better, Miss Henrietta."

She whimpered as he put is hands around her throat, and sobbed when he dropped them with a laugh. "Perhaps, in fact, it would be more amusing to be the one to make public *your* peccadilloes. What do you think people will say when they hear you came to visit me here alone? A woman who's lost her virtue has little credibility in the eyes of a critical society."

"The only one who's lost credibility is you, Debenham!" Through the door burst her husband, snarling the rejoinder as Hetty struggled in her assailant's embrace.

"Sir Aubrey!" she wept, relief swamping her as she reached out her arms.

His joyful expression sustained her for a moment. Then Debenham threw her roughly back against the wall before bending to snatch up the glass that had contained his arrack. In one smooth, sudden action, he smashed it upon the low table, brandishing the jagged base as he spun to seize Hetty 'round the neck once more.

"Hetty!" Araminta wailed as she flew into the room in Sir Aubrey's wake.

Lord Debenham, still pinioning Hetty against the wall, raised an eyebrow. "Miss Partington, how delightful that you made our assignation at last. So you've come to give me the letter in return for the release of our little hostage?"

The fearful gaze Araminta turned upon Sir Aubrey was, Hetty suspected, more on her own account than Hetty's. "I don't know what you mean," she whispered.

Hetty made a strangled noise. "Araminta, you took the letter, I know you did!"

Araminta shook her head. "I...I hid it," she said

unconvincingly.

Sir Aubrey stepped forward, his eyes boring into Hetty's, offering her the courage she needed as he said, "I couldn't care less what becomes of the letter. All I want is Hetty's freedom."

Araminta's satisfied laugh turned all eyes on her as she said, "Well, that's easy then—for I have the letter. Now all I need is an offer of marriage from Sir Aubrey and I'll happily hand it over."

Lord Debenham, with a disgusted snort, thrust Hetty away. Quickly she ran to the sanctuary of her beloved's embrace, resting her head against his hard chest as his arms banded about her. The relief of finding safety was heightened by the satisfaction in his voice.

"I'm afraid that even if I had the slightest desire to accede to your threats, Miss Partington—which I do not—your demands are impossible to fulfill. Your sister and I were married less than an hour ago by special license."

"No!" Araminta's shriek was a joy to listen to.

Hetty glanced up at Sir Aubrey as he drew her in tighter, and she saw all the love she felt for him reflected in his answering expression.

Like Hetty, he clearly felt no sympathy for Araminta, who held her hands to her face as she sank upon the cushions, wailing, "Tell me it's a lie, Henrietta! Tell me you would never be so underhanded!"

Hetty was happy to show open exultation at that. "Underhanded, Araminta? I cannot see how you'd think my actions underhanded when they are more than equaled by your own. Nevertheless, it's true. I became Sir Aubrey's wife moments before I came here to claim the letter."

Lord Debenham fixed his malevolent gaze upon her sister. His lips twitched and Hetty knew she should perhaps feel a twinge of concern on Araminta's behalf but, she consoled herself, her new husband had already shown he knew how to keep order.

He spoke now, his eyes warm as they rested on her. "My Henrietta has shown the most enormous courage and astonishing loyalty toward me." Hetty felt she'd never been happier in her life as he went on. "I'm sorry, Miss Partington, but your devious behavior tonight has only proved how much worthier your younger sister is of my enduring and heartfelt love and admiration."

Hetty, glowing, believed she could have listened to such

compliments uttered in the public domain forever. Clearly Araminta had heard enough, though, for she leapt forward, eyes blazing.

"What is this worth to you, Lord Debenham…Sir Aubrey?" she demanded, dipping her hand into her décolletage before brandishing the letter they'd been seeking.

Stepping backward, she lowered the parchment so that it hovered just above the guttering candle on the table by the window. "All of you have betrayed me. Hetty, you took what was rightfully mine. Lord Debenham," she spat, "I once considered you a worthy suitor but I'd not wish you on my worst enemy, knowing what a hateful, hideous creature you are."

Lord Debenham took a slow, calculated breath. His smile was evil. "You would do well to burn the letter, Miss Partington. It must have been a terrible shock to find yourself a victim of Sir Aubrey's disloyalty since he gave you every reason to believe he'd make you an honorable offer. No doubt you want to destroy that letter as much as you want to destroy the man who dashed your hopes."

It occurred to Hetty that Araminta might use the leverage of the letter to win Lord Debenham over, but Hetty certainly no longer cared. Sir Aubrey could not have made clearer the sincerity of his feelings, and she knew that with time, he'd earn back the respect of the public through his own efforts. He'd already proved himself a decent and honorable man.

She turned expectantly towards the door, surprised when her husband hesitated. She glanced up at him, then over at the table where her sister stood.

"Miss Partington." Sir Aubrey fixed Araminta with a gaze of such warmth and appreciation, Hetty tensed to contain her jealousy. But then he went on. "No amount of inducement or blackmail is more important to me than securing my happiness through Hetty's consent to be my wife tonight. The ink is dry on the special license, and shortly I will inform Lord Partington of the happy state of affairs. Do what you will, for I am about to take my wife…home."

Hetty returned the pressure of her husband's hand, shivering with anticipation at the thought of what being taken "home" actually meant.

Araminta looked panicked. Hovering over the candle, waving the letter that neither man wanted enough that he was prepared to accede to her demands, must have been galling.

"The marriage is not yet registered!"

Hetty smiled at Araminta, who was clearly clutching at straws as her sister went on, shrilly, "You can burn the special license and there's still time to stop the clergyman before he puts it in the register."

Sir Aubrey cocked his head. "Why would I want to do that? I have the wife I want."

"But your reputation, Sir Aubrey...you do not have that, and I can return it to you by giving you this letter."

"Your demands are too great, Miss Partington. I shall leave you here now with Lord Debenham. You are in good company." He stroked Hetty's cheek then turned back to Araminta. "If we're worried about reputations, Miss Partington, I'd suggest yours is in the greatest danger, so perhaps it's best if you followed us and we'll return you to your cousins."

"No, Sir Aubrey! Too much is at stake! I know too much and you'd do well to do as I say!"

Hetty had never seen Araminta so wild. Her desperation was like a soothing balm for all the years of slights and insults she'd had suffered at her sister's hands.

"Come back with us, Araminta," she said, feeling suddenly charitable, enjoying the warmth of her husband's dependable bulk pressed against her side. "I hate to see you so upset."

"Of course I'm upset. Sir Aubrey! You can't just leave!"

Sir Aubrey turned back from his progress towards the door and Hetty bit her lip as she watched him fix his considered gaze upon Araminta. But there was no suggestion he felt even a modicum of kindliness towards her. His eyes were as cold as she'd ever seen them.

"You have not done well this night, sister-in-law. Do what you will, and consider well what you have done, but I warn you, you shall be responsible for bearing your own burdens." He reached down to cup Hetty's cheek, his eyes suddenly misting as he murmured, "I am proud to have won the affections of such an honorable woman. A woman I do not deserve but who I consider it the greatest honor to call my wife."

A feeling of the greatest delight and warmth wrapped around Hetty's heart and settled in the pit of her stomach but she still felt a sense of responsibility.

"Please, Araminta, reconsider," she begged, extending her hand to her sister, who jerked backward and touched the tip of the letter to the flame.

"I *shall* do it!" Araminta screeched.

Hetty glanced up. Sir Aubrey seemed unaffected by the imminent torching of his reputation while Lord Debenham lounged against the window sill, watching the proceedings with what seemed like great satisfaction.

Hetty tried one final gambit. "Araminta, you are thwarting justice if you carry through on your threats. It's too late. Sir Aubrey and I are legally married."

"It's not too late!" Araminta hissed.

Sir Aubrey took another couple of steps toward the door and Hetty followed, clinging to his arm. "Come with us, Araminta," she entreated, over her shoulder. "You can't stay here, alone. If you don't find a husband in your second season, there's always a third. It's not until the end of a third failed season that all is lost." She couldn't help offering her sister the same reassurance Araminta had continually dished out to her. "At least, that's what you've always told me."

Araminta glared and Hetty looked up to catch the smile her new husband directed towards her. Wonderingly, she touched the streak of white hair amidst the dark that characterized the men of his family. Her child, if it were a son, would carry that same badge of honor, for Hetty intended, as his wife and hostess, to see that Sir Aubrey regained the status he deserved.

"There! It's alight!"

The smell of burning parchment came as no surprise. Hetty knew that Araminta, ever spiteful, would not be won over by truth and justice. What was surprising was the lack of concern on her husband's face.

Less surprising was the satisfaction on Lord Debenham's whose mouth was turned up like a satyr's as he watched from the shadows.

Sir Aubrey bent his head low to put his lips to Hetty's ear. "We must leave if we are to make the crossing to France in the morning," and Hetty sighed rapturously. "A proper elopement. How thrilling!"

Resting her head briefly against his chest, her attention was diverted by Araminta's cry. She turned and saw her sister's face contort with pain as the flames licked the corners of the parchment to reach up for her fingers.

Araminta released the charred remains with a gasp of satisfaction, her expression marred by malice.

For the first time Hetty was not afraid of what she might do next. Araminta was a spent force. Hetty had the man of her dreams, a man united with her in body and soul, and nothing Araminta said or did could hurt her now. She made one final attempt to persuade Araminta of reason, extending her arm toward her, but Araminta recoiled. Sighing, Hetty shrugged. "Tonight has not gone as you'd planned, Araminta, but only you will suffer," she said, turning upon the threshold. "You have not made me proud but as your sister, you will always have my loyalty for you and I are bound by blood ties."

With a final glance between her darling husband who was gazing at her with undisguised affection, and her fulminating sister, Hetty was about to say more when Sir Aubrey cut in, drawing her into the circle of his embrace as he finished telling Araminta, "Whereas your sister and I are bound by mutual love and respect."

Words that resonated throughout her whole body as he emphasized them with a heartfelt kiss.

The End

What Happens Next?

The Daughters of Sin series follows the intertwining lives and sibling rivalry of Lord Partington's two nobly born—and two illegitimate—daughters as they compete for love during several London Seasons.

Hetty and Araminta's lives are now bound up with two men on opposing sides of a dastardly plot that is being investigated by Stephen Cranbourne, a secret agent in the Foreign Office.

When their half-sister, Lissa, a governess, is recruited to the cause on account of her skilful character sketches, loyalties are further divided. With lashings of skullduggery and intrigue bound up in the central romance, and sibling rivalry between three very different, ambitious young ladies, there's lots of angst, however true hearts prevail.

And, just in case you're ever worried that someone doesn't get their happy ending, or just desserts—rest assured that they will do, either in their book, or by the end of the series.

What Readers are Saying About the Series:

"…lies, misdeeds, treachery, and romance. What an impressive story! Ms. Oakley has a unique way of telling her stories, bringing unknown heroes/ heroines into the spotlight, as they navigate a world of espionage, and intrigue, all while trying to survive and find their HEA. Magnificent and mesmerizing!" ~ **Amazon reader**

"Full of secrets, murders, intrigues and you feel you know the characters and want to strangle some of them, especially Araminta!!! I have since read all in the series and can't wait for Book 5... This is a series I will read again and again." ~ **Amazon reader**

Below is the order of the books:

HER GILDED PRISON (Book 1)

She was determined to secure the succession, he was in it for the pleasure. Falling in love was not part of the arrangement.

***

When dashing twenty-five-year-old Stephen Cranbourne arrives at the estate he will one day inherit, it's expected he will make a match with his beautiful second cousin, Araminta. But while proud, fiery Araminta and her shy, plain sister, Hetty, parade their very different charms before him, it's their mother, Sybil, a lonely and discarded wife, who evokes first his sympathy and then stokes his lustful fires.

DANGEROUS GENTLEMEN

Shy, plain Hetty was the wallflower beneath his notice…until a terrible mistake has one dangerous, delicious rake believing she's the "fair Cyprian" ordered for his pleasure.

Shy, self-effacing Henrietta knows her place—in her dazzling older sister's shadow. She's a little brown peahen to Araminta's bird of paradise. But when Hetty mistakenly becomes embroiled in the Regency underworld, the innocent debutante finds herself shockingly compromised by the dashing, dangerous Sir Aubrey, the very gentleman her heart desires. And the man Araminta has in her cold, calculating sights.

Branded an enemy of the Crown, bitter over the loss of his wife, Sir Aubrey wants only to lose himself in the warm, willing body of the young "prostitute" Hetty. As he tutors her in the art of lovemaking, Aubrey is pleased to find Hetty not only an ardent student, but a bright, witty and charming companion.

Despite a spoiled Araminta plotting for a marriage offer and a powerful political enemy damaging his reputation, Aubrey may suffer the greatest betrayal at the hands of the little "concubine" who's managed to breach the stony exterior of his heart.

Lissa Hazlett lives life in the shadows. The beautiful, illegitimate daughter of Viscount Partington earns her living as an overworked governess while her vain and spoiled half sister, Araminta, enjoys London's social whirl as its most feted debutante.

When Lissa's rare talent as a portraitist brings her unexpectedly into the bosom of society – and into the midst of a scandal involving Araminta and suspected English traitor Lord Debenham – she finds an unlikely ally: charming and besotted Ralph Tunley, Lord Debenham's underpaid, enterprising secretary.

BEYOND RUBIES

Fame. Fortune. And finally a marriage proposal!

Book 4 of the Daughters of Sin series introduces Miss Kitty La Bijou, celebrated London actress, mistress to handsome Lord Nash and the unacknowledged illegitimate daughter of Viscount Partington.

Having escaped her humble beginnings, Kitty has found fame, fortune and love, but the respectability she craves eludes her. When she stumbles across Araminta, her legitimate half-sister, on the verge of giving birth just seven months after marrying dangerous Viscount Debenham, Kitty realises respectability is no guarantee of character or happiness.

But helping Araminta has unwittingly embroiled Kitty in a scandalous deception involving a ruthless brothel madam, a priceless ruby necklace and the future heir to a dazzling fortune.

And when Kitty finally receives an offer of marriage she must choose. Respectability or love?

LADY UNVEILED ~ THE CUCKOLD CONSPIRACY

Kitty has the love of the man of her dreams but as London's most acclaimed actress and a member of the demimondaine, she accepts she can never be kind and handsome Lord Silverton's lawful wedded wife.

When Kitty comes to the aid of shy, accident-prone and kind-hearted Octavia Mandelton, her sense of justice leads to her making the most difficult decision of her life: Give up the man she loves for the sake of honour. For Octavia is still betrothed to Lord Silverton who'd rescued Kitty in dramatic circumstances only weeks before.

Cast adrift, Kitty joins forces with her sister, Lissa, a talented artist posing as a governess in order to bring to justice a dangerous spy, villainous Lord Debenham. Complicating matters is the fact Debenham is married to their half-sister, vain and beautiful Araminta.

However, Araminta has a dark secret which only Kitty knows and which she realizes she is duty-bound to expose if she's to achieve justice and win happiness for deserving Lissa and Lissa's enterprising sweetheart, Ralph Tunley, long-suffering secretary to Lord Debenham.

All seems set for a happy ending when Kitty tumbles into mortal danger. A danger from which only a truly honorable man can save her. A man like Silverton who must now make the hardest choice of his life if he's to live with his conscience.

Want to read the next two books in the series, and save?
If you've read book 1, you can get Books 2 and 3, discounted in a Box Set.

In Dangerous Gentlemen, Sweet, shy Hetty finds herself in competition with her beautiful, spoiled sister, Araminta, as they both hope for a marriage offer. In The Mysterious Governess, the girls' unacknowledged half-sister, Lissa, a governess, uses her sketching ability to help apprehend a dangerous spy.

The First Three Books in the Series - Her Gilded Prison, Dangerous Gentlemen and The Mysterious Governess – are also contained in a box set. Buy all together, and save!

ABOUT THE AUTHOR

Beverley was seventeen when she bundled up her first 500+ page romance and sent it to a publisher. Rejection followed swiftly. Drowning one's heroine on the last page, she was informed, was not in line with the expectations of romance readers.

So Beverley became a journalist.

After a whirlwind romance with a handsome Norwegian bush pilot she met in Botswana, Beverley discovered her "Happy Ever After", and her first romance was published in 2009.

Since then, she's written more than fifteen sizzling historical romances laced with mystery and intrigue under the name Beverley Oakley.

She also writes psychological historicals, and Colonial-Africa-set romantic suspense, as Beverley Eikli.

With an inspiring view of a Gothic nineteenth-century insane asylum across the road, Beverley lives north of Melbourne with her gorgeous husband, two lovely daughters and rambunctious Rhodesian Ridgeback, Mombo, named after the Okavango Delta safari lodge where she and her husband met.

You can find out more at www.beverleyoakley.com or follow her on Facebook at
https://www.facebook.com/AuthorBeverleyOakley/

Printed in Great Britain
by Amazon

55391023R00108